A

'Do you hate all men, or just me in particular?'

'I hate what you're doing to a vulnerable, fatherless boy, who's as fragile as glass right now.'

Jonah's mouth held a sardonic twist. 'Do you intend to make Brody wallow for years on end in your morbid widow's grief?'

'*How dare you*?'

'Oh, I dare, lady,' he ground out. 'I haven't even started.'

Dear Reader

Welcome to our exciting mini-series—**Sealed with a Kiss.** Every month we'll be featuring a romance sparked off by a letter, an advertisement—or even a diary. Some of the world's greatest romances have begun in writing... and ended with a marriage licence! This is a tradition continued by ten of our popular authors—each and every one of whom has brought her own unique style to the romance.

We hope that you enjoy this **Sealed with a Kiss** title and all the other terrific romances that we have out this month!

The Editors

Rebecca Winters, an American writer and mother of four, is a graduate of the University of Utah. She has also studied at schools in Switzerland and France, including the Sorbonne. Rebecca is currently teaching French and Spanish to junior high-school students. Despite her busy schedule, Rebecca always finds time to write. She's already researching the background for her next romance!

Recent titles by the same author:

BLIND TO LOVE
THE RANCHER AND THE REDHEAD

RETURN TO SENDER

BY
REBECCA WINTERS

MILLS & BOON

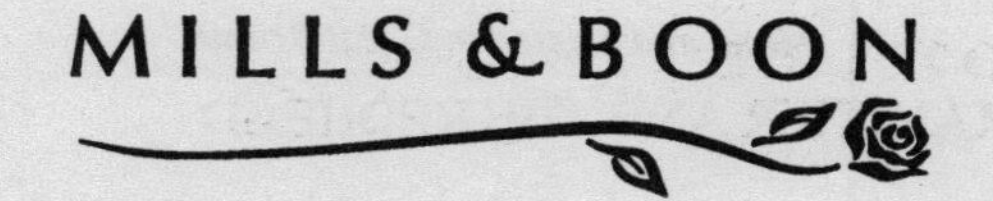

Harlequin Mills & Boon Limited,
Eton House, 18-24 Paradise Road, Richmond, Surrey TW9 1SR
This edition published by arrangement with
Harlequin Enterprises B.V.

ISBN 0 263 79238 2

Set in Times Roman 11 on 12 pt.
01-9510-45000 C1

Made and printed in Great Britain

CHAPTER ONE

Dear Mrs Brown,

Am arranging a flight from San Diego to arrive in Denver August nineteenth. Regret I cannot give you a definite time yet. Will take a taxi from the airport.

Jonah Sinclair.

SARAH moaned. For a fraction of a second, she'd thought...

'What's the matter, Mom?'

Sarah Brown eyed her troubled seven-year-old son, Brody. Though he took after her, with his dark hair and blue eyes, he'd been born with Rich's slight build and nervous energy. Sometimes that energy drove her to distraction—like now.

Instead of being over at the pool with the other kids for his swimming lesson, he sat impatiently at the dining-room table, getting into her things while he watched her work on some research.

She finally gave up, realizing she'd have to finish this project after he'd gone to bed, which posed a further problem because he rarely fell asleep before midnight.

'I—— It's nothing, honey. I seem to have opened someone else's mail again.' Because there was a

Birchwood North and a Birchwood South, every so often the mailman delivered a letter to the wrong Mrs Richard Brown. But this one had a San Diego postmark... How strange.

'Will they get mad?'

'I don't think so, because it's not my fault. There's a woman who lives in the Birchwood South condos with the same name as ours. I've gotten her mail before.'

'Where are you going?' He dropped what he was doing and followed her to the phone in the kitchen. Her shadow.

He'd been like this since the beginning of the summer, preferring to stay with her every day rather than play and do all the normal things a boy his age liked to do.

The only relief came when she could get Jeff, one of the boys his age who lived in a nearby condo, to spend a morning or afternoon with him. But, more often than not, they ended up fighting. Brody didn't seem to care if Jeff went home mad, stating that they weren't best friends.

When Sarah discussed her worry over Brody's abnormal behavior with Jeff's mother, Patsy, the other woman suggested that it was possible Brody was missing his old neighborhood and friends.

Sarah secretly wondered the same thing. While her husband, Rich, had served in the coast guard, they'd lived in San Diego. But, twenty months ago, a storm at sea on Christmas Eve had taken his life along with six other men, none of whose bodies had been found. Intellectually, Sarah knew he was dead. But an irrational part of her didn't quite believe it.

She was angry. Angry that his need for adventure had resulted in catastrophe, depriving her and Brody of the husband and father they'd loved.

Since then, her lifestyle had changed drastically. No longer able to be a full-time mother, who had the luxury of staying home with her son, she'd been forced to go to work, because the little savings she and Rich had accrued wouldn't last long.

She had got her old job back at the law firm where she'd been a legal researcher before she'd had Brody. But between the expenses of day-to-day living, along with car payments, insurance, taxes, and the necessity of paying a woman to watch Brody every day after school until Sarah got home from work, she had barely been making it financially.

When the landlord had raised the rent on her apartment complex, she knew she was in trouble and had started looking for a cheaper place to live.

Then, as if in answer to prayer, her sister, Valerie, who lived in Denver, had asked Sarah if she would consider moving there to house-sit their luxury condo while she and her husband moved to the Far East with his engineering company for a year.

They didn't want to sell their condo, but they didn't want the wrong people renting from them—Hal was adamant about no smoking and no pets. Since Sarah had never smoked and didn't own a pet, they'd asked her to think about pulling up stakes and moving. They'd make the house payments every month if she could pay for everything else.

Sarah considered it a gift from heaven, jumping at the chance to help her sister and brother-in-law. Not only would there be opportunities to do legal research in Denver, but by a year's time she would have saved enough money to find a rental she could afford in a decent neighborhood and still be close to her sister.

With their parents deceased, after a train accident years earlier, her elder sister, Valerie, was the only family she had left.

Rich's parents came from high society on the east coast. When he had left home to find his own way in the world, his parents had disowned him for not following in his father's footsteps. The only time Sarah had met them was at the memorial service held for Rich and the men who had died serving their country.

In fairness to his parents, they had obviously been grief-stricken. But they had looked at Sarah and Brody as if she and their grandson had sprung from some alien planet. Without a pedigree that dated back to the Mayflower, Sarah had no validity in their eyes.

From the first moment they'd met they had conveyed their disapproval, and seemed to blame her in some way for their son's rejection of them, for his need to live life on the edge—a life that had been permanently snuffed out.

As far as Sarah was concerned, they were monsters. For herself, she didn't care if they refused to acknowledge her. But for them to ignore Brody, as if he didn't exist, was something she would never fathom or forgive. In consequence, she tried to pour out her love to her son by being all things to him—mother, father, and doting grandparent.

In retrospect, she realized that because of her grief and continual worries over money, she hadn't considered what a change in residence and location might do to Brody. The apartment in San Diego had been his home since birth.

Could Patsy be right? Had the move been too traumatic for him? Sarah agonized.

As she hunted for the other Mrs Brown's number among all the Richard Browns in the telephone directory her gaze wandered to her restless son, who had difficulty concentrating on any task for very long. Like Rich, he needed to stay busy or he was bored. But lately Sarah had had trouble keeping Brody interested in anything.

'There doesn't seem to be a listing for a Mrs Richard Brown at Birchwood South. I was hoping she'd come and get her mail this time. Since that's out, we'd better take it over to her now. From the sound of it, she's expecting company tomorrow.'

'Wait till I get my roller blades,' Brody announced.

She started to say something, but it was too late. He'd already disappeared into the bedroom. She hated roller blades; they were too dangerous. But it seemed that every child in Birchwood owned a pair. After a month of Brody's endless begging and pleading, she'd finally relented and bought him some. They had had to be pink and black.

'Be sure and put on your pads and helmet.'

'Ah, Mom—none of the kids wear all that stuff.'

'Maybe their parents can afford hospital bills. I can't.'

'Are we poor?'

'No,' she lied, not wanting to burden him with her problems. 'I just love you too much to see you get hurt.'

Beneath the rim of his baseball cap she saw his eyes trained soulfully up at her. 'I was wondering if you'd feel bad if I died.'

'Brody!' she cried out, horrified. On a rush of emotion, she picked him up and held him for a long time. 'How could you ask me a question like that? I was the happiest mom in the world when you were born.' After putting him down she said, 'But I'm worried because you're not over at the pool.'

'I don't like to swim.'

'You used to when your d——' She stopped herself, but it was too late. She'd done it again. Bringing up the past would only make matters worse.

Heaving a weary sigh she said, 'I'll tell you what. You don't have to swim if you don't want to. We'll have fun around here. Just think, school starts in a week.'

'I hate school,' he muttered.

At that new revelation, a shudder ran through Sarah. One more problem to deal with.

'That was last year,' she improvised. 'Next week you're starting second grade in a brand new school, where a lot of the kids will be new, too. Remember Mrs Ruff, the lady you met when we went over there in June to get you registered? She's going to be your teacher, and she was so nice to you and showed you your room. Things will be different this year, just wait and see.'

'I still don't want to go.'

Taking a fortifying breath she said, 'Go get your equipment on, honey, or you'll have to leave the blades at home.'

'Okay,' he mumbled, glum-faced, and set them on the kitchen floor before he went back to his room for everything else.

At this point Sarah was glad to have a reason to get out of the house. A walk through the complex to the other one across the street would be therapeutic for her and good for Brody, who needed to work off his excess energy and stop dwelling on the negative.

While Brody fastened his blades Sarah waited on the porch with the letter in hand. The blazing sun had turned the afternoon into another scorcher. Eight days of temperatures above ninety-five degrees.

This latest bout of heat was too much. She hoped the weatherman was right. Some time tomorrow they were supposed to be getting a huge electrical storm with heavy rain showers. She looked forward to the change. Maybe cooler temperatures would entice Brody out of the house and wash away the gloom which seemed to have descended upon her in suffocating waves.

She used to love summer, but not anymore. Damn you, Rich, for doing this to us, she cried inwardly. It seemed as if, in the last year, anger over the senseless loss had tended to swamp her pangs of sorrow, robbing her of the *joie de vivre* she'd once thought inherent in her nature.

'Mom? Aren't you through yet?'

Embarrassed by her son's outburst, Sarah turned to the young, wiry attorney who, on urgent business, had driven over to the condo in the rain to bring her some work he needed researched as soon as possible.

'Excuse me, please. I'll be right back.'

She didn't have to go far. Brody stood waiting for her in the hallway off the living-room. She'd put him to bed an hour ago and had even read part of *The Boxcar Children* to him.

'How many times have we had this conversation before, Brody? You mustn't disturb me while I have a client here. What is it now?'

'I can't sleep. The thunder's too loud.'

Thunder had never bothered Brody before. This was just an excuse to get her to himself. Lately he had seemed to resent any attorneys who came to the door dropping off case material.

Thinking fast, she said, 'Go get in my bed and turn on the TV. Mr Belnap won't be here much longer.'

'Promise?'

His wistful expression tugged at her heart. She put her arms around him and hugged him hard. 'Yes, honey.'

Reassured, he squeezed her back, then headed in the direction of her room. She waited until he'd disappeared before she rejoined Mr Belnap with an apology. After listening to what he wanted her to do, she assured him she would get on it first thing in the morning. Then she bid him goodnight and opened the door for him.

The rain was coming down in torrents. He used his suit coat and briefcase for an umbrella and dashed out to his car, parked at the front curb.

No sooner had Sarah shut the door behind him and put the material on the dining-room table than the buzzer sounded again.

'Mom?'

'Just a minute, Brody!' she called out in frustration, and hurried over to the entry again. She couldn't believe Mr Belnap would come back in this rain. Apparently he'd forgotten to tell her something of extreme importance.

With his name on her lips, she opened the door once more. But her words ended on a slight gasp as a flash of lightning illuminated the sky, outlining the figure of a well-honed, masculine physique backed by a curtain of rain.

The stranger, dressed in what looked like hip-hugging jeans and sweatshirt, couldn't possibly be Mr Belnap, or any other attorney of her acquaintance. Maybe it was her imagination, but, in that brief second, she sensed an aura of power emanating from the man, who looked to be in his thirties and stood over six feet tall—much taller than Rich, who'd been just the right size for her five-feet-five frame.

'Y-Yes?' she finally asked, holding on to the door as if for protection. 'May I help you?'

'I'm looking for Mrs Brown.' The deep, resonant voice permeated to her fingertips. Everything about the man seemed vibrantly alive and made an indelible impression. For some unaccountable reason it disturbed her, especially the way his gaze studied her heavily lashed Venetian-blue eyes and shoulder-length black hair for an overly long moment.

'I'm Mrs Brown.'

A sudden stillness pervaded the atmosphere and another flash of lightning bathed them like the noonday sun, revealing his arresting features and fairly short dark blond hair. His eyes looked black, but were probably brown.

One brow dipped. 'Mrs *Richard* Brown?'

'Yes,' she said, feeling a trifle impatient that he sounded so skeptical. His eyes played over her face and body with a brooding intensity, robbing her of breath.

'I was led to believe you were a woman in her late seventies.'

In truth, since Rich's death there'd been times when she'd felt that old. In fact, during the first month after the memorial service, she'd found herself wishing all three of them could have died together so there'd be no more pain.

After a tension-filled pause the stranger added, 'Obviously the man was blind.'

The slight quirk of his compelling mouth and his slow male scrutiny of her feminine attributes caught Sarah off-guard and made her blush, something she'd never done before, not even when she'd first met Rich.

Clearing her throat, she said, 'Can I help you, Mr——?'

'Sinclair. Jonah Sinclair.'

Sinclair. She blinked. She'd heard that name before. 'Oh!' she cried out, suddenly remembering. 'You're the man who wrote the letter saying you'd be arriving today.'

'Good.' He nodded in satisfaction. 'I'm glad you got it in time.'

'No——' she blurted out. 'I didn't——' She rubbed her palms against her hips, a gesture he followed with his eyes, confusing her because everything he said and did seemed so intimate somehow.

'I mean, I did get it, but it wasn't meant for me. I opened it by mistake. But I took it right over to Mrs Brown's and put it in her mailbox.'

His expression was thoroughly puzzled. 'You're Mrs Richard Brown, and you live at 455C?'

She moistened her lips, which had gone dry. 'Yes, but you're in the wrong complex. The Mrs Brown you're looking for lives in 455C across the street in Birchwood South.'

This time he blinked. 'My realtor didn't say anything about two complexes. I'm from San Diego and I've had to rely on him to make all my arrangements.'

'Mom? When are you coming?' Brody sounded upset.

'In a minute, honey.' Eyeing the stranger again, she apologized for Brody and said, 'If your realtor thought there was only one Mrs Richard Brown, he probably didn't see the need to make the distinction.'

'From the sounds of it, this has happened to you more than once. I'm sorry to have disturbed you and your family. Thank you for your help. Goodnight.'

'Goodbye.' She shut the door, glad he was gone. Since Rich's death, she'd been dead as far as any interest in other men had been concerned. Yet this total stranger had had a way of looking at her that disturbed her equilibrium, forcing her to be aware of him as a man whose appeal was not only alarming, but, she feared, unforgettable.

It seemed such a betrayal of Rich's memory. That was what was troubling her. The stranger had mentioned a realtor. She hoped it didn't mean what she was thinking...

After locking up and turning out the lights, she joined Brody in the bedroom and got ready for bed. Once they were both tucked in, he fell asleep with his hand touching her arm. She didn't have the heart to move him.

Knowing he needed rest, she edged away from him and clung to her side of the bed, closing her eyes to better remember what life had been like when Rich had been the one holding her. But her anger kept getting in the way of those sweet dreams.

Sarah had never been able to relate to Rich's willingness to put his life in jeopardy. In that regard, she wasn't any different from his parents, except that she'd tried hard not to make it an issue.

But tonight her mind went back to the arguments they'd had before he'd left on his last tour of duty, when she'd accused him of not loving her and Brody enough to quit the coast guard. Those were the only ugly memories of their marriage.

Except for his career, Sarah had had few complaints. When he had been home, she had loved cooking meals for him while they watched the ball games together. Throughout their marriage she'd kept her job as a legal researcher, which allowed her to do a lot of the work at their apartment, thus affording them more time together when he was in port.

Of course, everything had changed when Brody came along. She'd quit her job to take care of him and had hoped Rich would start thinking about quitting the coast guard to do some other less life-threatening kind of work.

As always, her thoughts led her to the horror of what it must have been like for him and his buddies when they were swallowed up in that storm. For months she'd had nightmares, where she would swim frantically in a dark sea filled with sharks, looking for his body, never finding it.

For the most part, the nightmares had ended, but she couldn't help but mourn because there was no hallowed spot marking his grave, where she and Brody could take flowers and remember him.

Thank heaven she'd kept photo albums. Right now she needed to look in them again, as she'd done on countless occasions with Brody. For a little while, studying Rich's face with his dancing blue eyes and sunny smile took away the haunting specter of his death and banished the intrusion of the stranger from her mind.

Leaving Brody in a sound sleep, she slipped quietly from the bed and padded out into the hall. On impulse, she made a detour to the kitchen for a soda, then went to the living-room where she turned on the light and ensconced herself on the couch.

When the front buzzer sounded, she couldn't believe it. Her watch said ten to twelve. She absolutely refused to open the door to anyone this late. Who would be out in this downpour?

Soon she heard knocking and got to her feet, wondering what person besides the manager would have the audacity to waken her at this time of night. In any event, the manager would have phoned first.

'Mrs Brown?'

Sarah recognized that low, vibrant voice. Her hands trembled as she put the albums back on the table. By now Brody had joined her and she put her arm around his shoulders, whispering to her son to be quiet.

The man knocked harder and rang the buzzer again. 'Mrs Brown? Are you there? It's Jonah Sinclair.'

Brody looked up at her. 'That's the man who was here earlier,' he said with unabashed honesty, which meant he'd been watching and listening from the hallway all evening. 'Why don't you let him in, Mom? It's still raining!'

Hating this entire situation, Sarah called out, 'Yes? What is it?'

'I'm sorry for disturbing you, but I saw a light go on. Could you phone for a taxi for me? Mrs Brown wasn't home and the manager doesn't answer. I left a message on his voice mail, but I'm afraid that's not going to help me. The office is locked. In a residential area like this, I have no idea where to find a payphone this time of night.'

'You can use ours!'

'*Brody*!'

But he broke away from Sarah too fast and had the door unlocked before she could stop him.

In the next instant her shocked gaze took in Jonah Sinclair's drenched appearance, while his all-encompassing eyes swept over the full curves of her body dressed in a summery nightgown which left little to the imagination.

She shrieked and disappeared down the hall, so furious at Brody that she was ready to strangle her own flesh and blood.

Grabbing for the first thing she could find to cover herself completely, she threw on her ankle-length quilted robe, the one she reserved for freezing winter nights. When every button had been fastened, she went back to the living-room, knowing her cheeks matched the color of the red plaid material.

To her surprise, Brody was alone in the living-room and the front door had been shut and locked.

'Mom——' Brody rushed over to her. 'I'm sorry I did that. Mr Sinclair told me I should never open the door to anyone, even if I thought you knew them.'

It would be pointless to remind Brody that she'd been drumming that particular piece of advice into his head since he was old enough to answer the door. Why was it that this particular man could drive the lesson home so it finally made an impact?

More threatened than ever by the stranger's unexpected advent in their lives, she demanded a trifle harshly, 'Where did he go?'

'I think he's still on the porch. Are you going to let him in?'

'I don't very well have a choice, do I?' she muttered under her breath, as upset with their nocturnal visitor as she was with her impulsive, headstrong son.

Unable to put off the inevitable any longer, she unlocked the door and opened it. Jonah Sinclair was lounging negligently against a pillar of the Georgian-style townhouse, his strong arms folded across his chest. The storm had passed over and the rain had started to let up, but he was obviously soaked to the skin, which for some reason only seemed to add to his attractiveness.

Avoiding his eyes she said, 'Come in, Mr Sinclair.'

'That won't be necessary, Mrs Brown. I apologize for disturbing you again. If it wouldn't put you out too much to call for a taxi, I'd be grateful.'

'I'll be happy to do that for you, but you're wringing wet. I doubt the driver will let you get in his cab in your condition. Come into the kitchen and I'll put your clothes in the dryer while you wait.'

After a brief pause, he did her bidding and followed her inside the condo. While she shut the door Brody showed him through the living and dining-area to the kitchen.

'You can wear my dad's robe,' she heard her son offer.

'You don't think he'll mind?'

'Nope. My dad's dead.'

Stunned by Brody's matter-of-fact reply, Sarah didn't want to hear the rest of her son's explanation, nor did she want to hear the other man's response. She ran down the hall to the bedroom, where she reached for the phone directory and called the first cab company listed in the yellow pages. The sooner he left, the better.

Once that was accomplished, she went over to her closet, where she kept some of Rich's things because she still couldn't part with them.

None of his clothes would fit Jonah Sinclair's physique. Even Brody had figured that out, which was why she finally reached for the blue terry-cloth bathrobe she'd given Rich years earlier. It was large and had always been his favorite item to lounge in.

As loath as she was for their uninvited guest to wear it, she couldn't see anything else in the closet which would halfway cover him.

'Brody?' she called to her son from the doorway.

He came running down the hall. 'Yeah, Mom?' He was being unusually obedient and well-behaved, no doubt because he'd seen her set mouth and feared her wrath after Mr Sinclair left.

'Take this to him, and put his clothes in the dryer. When he's ready, let me know, and I'll come down and turn it on.'

'Okay. Mum—please don't be mad.' His voice shook.

'I'm not mad, Brody.'

'Yes, you are. You always get pink cheeks when you're mad. Jonah saw them, too. He said you should be mad at him, not me.' He reached for the robe and dashed back down the hall.

As if on cue, her face went hot.

So it was 'Jonah' already.

How dared a perfect stranger discuss anything with her son? Fired by indignation, she slammed the closet door and headed for the kitchen, intent on wresting Brody from that man's clutches and putting him to bed.

But she came to a complete standstill when she caught sight of Jonah Sinclair. She would never have recognized her husband's robe on him.

He was leaning over the chair where her son was seated, one hand on his young shoulder, his chin barely grazing his hair, patiently listening and making occasional comments as Brody showed him pictures of his father from the photo album. Flattered by this man's attention, her son sounded happier than she'd heard him since before Rich's death.

As Sarah's throat tightened from a *mélange* of conflicting emotions the stranger turned his head, and their eyes met in a long, unsmiling look. Slowly he stood up, filling her vision with his incredibly masculine essence.

Though not handsome in the classical sense, he possessed what Sarah could only describe as a rare male beauty, an elemental quality that went beneath the surface and struck a primitive chord in her so that she trembled.

CHAPTER TWO

'I TOOK the liberty of turning on your dryer.'

Now that he mentioned it, she could hear the sound coming from the laundry-room off the kitchen. Struggling for breath she said, 'That's good, because I've called for a taxi and it should be here any minute.'

'Oh, heck,' Brody grumbled. 'I was hoping he could stay with us tonight.'

Jonah Sinclair ruffled Brody's dark hair affectionately. 'Even if the circumstances were different and we were all good friends, I couldn't stay.' He pre-empted Sarah, who was still reeling from Brody's comment. Since Rich's death, he hadn't liked any man who paid the slightest attention to her. 'After I flew in from San Diego, I left my bags at the front desk of the Hilton and came directly here. I need to get back and check in.'

Brody jumped off the chair and stared up at him. 'Does it have a swimming-pool?'

'I think so.'

'Maybe I could come swimming with you tomorrow?'

'We have a perfectly good pool here, Brody,' she reminded him, in her most authoritative voice, before their guest could respond. 'Now, say goodbye to Mr Sinclair. You should have been in bed and asleep hours ago.'

His lower lip quivered and she could tell he was fighting tears.

What was it about this man that had produced such a profound effect on her son in so short a period of time? It didn't make sense. She resented the intrusion. She resented *him*.

'Brody?' she prodded.

'Goodbye, Jonah,' he whispered, and ran off, leaving Sarah to deal with an untenable situation.

'I'll check on your clothes.'

He didn't say anything, but as she went into the laundry-room she sensed his presence behind her, making her slightly claustrophobic in the tiny room. Opening the lid, she reached for his shirt and pants, which still felt a little damp.

'A-Another five minutes and they should be dry,' she said haltingly.

'I don't have five minutes. A horn just honked outside. I'll change in here and then be on my way.'

She nodded without looking at him. 'All right.' Reaching inside the dryer once more, she handed the clothes to him, then started to slip past him. In the process, the very thing she'd tried to avoid happened. Their thighs accidentally brushed against each other.

The brief contact spread liquid fire through her body, igniting something that had been lying dormant for so long, she'd almost forgotten what it felt like.

Terrified at the implication, she flew to the front door and turned on the porch light to let the cab driver know they'd heard his honk.

Within minutes Jonah Sinclair appeared in the living-room fully dressed. He moved in her direction, his intent gaze leveled on her flushed features. 'I'm indebted to you for your help,' he began in his deep voice. 'Say goodbye to Brody for me. He's a wonderful boy.'

'I think so,' she came back brusquely, smarting from the implied criticism that she didn't appreciate her son enough.

He frowned. 'Forgive me for intruding on your privacy twice in one night. You have my promise it won't happen again. Goodbye.'

She avoided his eyes and opened the door. 'Goodbye.'

The second he went outside, she shut it behind him and locked it. As soon as she heard the taxi pull away from the curb she turned off the porch light.

Thankful for that episode being over, she went to the kitchen to turn out the lights and saw the robe draped over one of the chairs.

When she plucked it from its resting place, she froze. The subtle scent of either the soap or the shaving lotion used by Jonah Sinclair still clung to the toweling, reminding her of that heartstopping moment when she'd been forced to squeeze past him. Another desecration of Rich's memory.

As if the material scorched her fingers, she went over to the waste-basket and dropped it inside.

'Why did you throw Dad's robe away, Mom?'

Sarah groaned and turned to her son, afraid of his reaction.

'Because it was old and worn out. I'm afraid it tore a little more when Mr Sinclair put it on.'

'I wish I was as tall as him.'

Staggered by the comment, because she'd thought Rich had been the only person on his mind, she said, 'You're just a boy, Brody. Some day you'll be as tall as your father.'

'But Dad was short.'

'He was five feet nine inches,' Sarah felt compelled to defend him. 'That's not short.'

'Jonah is six feet three inches, because I asked him. He's even bigger than Jeff's dad.'

Since when had height become an issue in her son's life? Damn Jonah Sinclair.

Flipping off the lights, she said, 'Come on. Let's go to bed.' She put a hand on his shoulder and they walked down the hall together.

'Thanks for letting him come in the house and get dry, Mom. He said he had jet-lag and was real tired.'

'I wonder if there's anything you two didn't discuss,' she muttered with ill-humor, and helped him get into his own bed. But, judging by Brody's next question, her comment had gone right over his head.

Gazing up at her with earnest eyes, he said, 'Do you think we'll ever see him again?'

She sincerely hoped not. 'No. I don't.' She smoothed the hair off his forehead. 'Brody, honey—why do you care? He's just a stranger who needed a ride back to his hotel.'

'He's nice. He told me his dad died before he was born, and he thought I was real lucky to be five years old before mine died. He said, now I'd always be able to remember how my dad laughed, what he said when he got mad, what he liked to eat for breakfast, how it felt when he hugged me. Stuff like that.' His little voice wobbled.

'He's right.' Sarah's voice shook. Despite her reservations about Jonah Sinclair, she marveled at his insight, and couldn't help wondering if he was a child psychologist or some such thing. 'We were both very lucky to have Daddy and love him for as long as we did.'

'Jonah said Dad was lucky to have us...' Brody's voice trailed off before he turned on his side and closed his eyes. 'Jonah said he'd be proud to have a son like me. He thinks I look like you.'

'That's because we have the same coloring.' She leaned over and kissed him goodnight, then headed for the door.

'Do you know what else he said?'

She shook her head in exasperation. 'No.' And she didn't want to know.

'He said he bet you were the most beautiful mom in Birchwood. I told him he was right. Jeff thinks so too. Goodnight, Mom.'

With pounding heart she whispered goodnight and walked straight to the formal dining-room, which she'd turned into an office while her sister and brother-in-law were away.

Right now she needed to get her mind off a certain enigmatic stranger. The best way to do that was to dig into the material Mr Belnap had brought over and outline the week's agenda.

Starting tomorrow, her research would take her to all the water-slide concessions in Denver and the surrounding area. One of them had been the scene of a recent drowning and the parents of the deceased child were bringing suit against the company responsible for the manufacture of the tube.

Sarah's job was to go down all the water-slides to make comparisons and observe the various safety features, if there were any. This was the kind of assignment Brody could do with her. They'd have a week of fun which would get them both out of the condo. Maybe Jeff could join them for a couple of those days.

She reached for the phone directory to look up all the addresses and plan the route she would take, making a mental note to call Patsy first thing in the morning.

After submerging herself in work for another hour, she finally felt tired enough to fall asleep and went to bed, praying that Brody would be excited about their plans.

She needn't have worried, because the next morning he woke up happier than she'd seen him in ages. She hated to admit it, but it looked as if Jonah Sinclair's comments had had a positive effect on Brody.

When she told him what they were going to be doing for the rest of the week, he let out a whoop and immediately asked if he could call Jeff. Soon Sarah talked to Patsy, and it was decided that after Jeff had finished his swimming lesson each day, he could go with them.

Thus started a busy week with the boys, and more carefree laughter than Sarah could remember in a long time. Doing things together while she gathered pertinent information for Mr Belnap seemed to bring Brody out of his shell. By the time the first day of school rolled around, she'd forgotten how intractable her son could be when he didn't want to do something.

'Brody? It's almost time. Breakfast is ready. I've made your favorite French toast. Come and get it!'

When he didn't respond, she walked down the hall, thinking he must be in the bathtub and couldn't hear her.

To her chagrin, she found him in bed, his face partially hidden by the pillow.

'Come on, Brody.' She removed the comforter. 'It's too late for a bath now. You're going to have to throw on your clothes or you'll be late for school.

Come on, sleepy-head,' she teased him, and jiggled his hip with her hand. 'Brody? I know you're awake. I can see your toes wiggling.'

He slowly removed the pillow and looked at her, his suntanned face wet with tears. Her spirits plummeted. 'I don't feel good.'

She sank down on the edge of the bed and squeezed his hand. 'I know you don't. That's why I'm going to go to school with you. If you want, I'll stay in the back of the class all day long.'

'No-o-o——' He rubbed his eyes. 'The kids will call me a sissy.'

She was ready for that. 'I bet there'll be a lot of moms there, not just me.'

'No there won't.'

She drew in a labored breath. 'Brody—if you had a son who didn't want to go to school, what would you do?'

'I wouldn't make him go.'

'And then he'd grow up not knowing how to read or write or do math. All the kids would make fun of him,' she said on a burst of inspiration. 'Is that what you'd want for your son?'

After a long silence he said, 'No.'

'I tell you what. I'll walk you to the front doors like all the other moms. When school's over, I'll be waiting on the sidewalk. You can either walk home with me or your friends. How's that?'

He started shaking his head and his face crumpled up. Before she knew it, he was crying. 'I hate school.'

Hardening her resolve, she said, 'Lots of kids feel the way you do. But once you get there, you'll like it.'

'I'll hate it!'

She cringed and got to her feet. 'Let's do this: at lunch, I'll come back to school and wait outside the doors. You can come out and tell me how it's going. If you still feel terrible, we'll go home for the rest of the day. But I'm asking you to give the morning a chance. Okay?'

It took him so long to answer, she thought he hadn't heard her. Finally, 'P-Promise to be there at lunch?'

'Don't I always keep my promises?'

He nodded.

'All right, then. Hurry and get your new clothes on. I'll warm up your French toast.'

'I'm not hungry.'

Her first impulse was to tell him he needed to start the day with a nourishing meal. But, on second thought, she decided she'd better not force the issue or he might change his mind on the other.

'It'll keep till lunch.'

But in that regard she was mistaken, because Brody didn't come home for lunch.

After writing a note to Mrs Ruff explaining the situation, Sarah went over to the school at eleven-thirty and waited a full hour for Brody to come out. He never did.

She didn't dare go inside—not even to the office—for fear she might upset him if he saw her.

On the other hand, she couldn't believe he wasn't at the door sobbing his heart out, as he'd been earlier that morning during the walk on the way over.

His red puffy face and tear-swollen eyes had haunted her morning and had made it impossible for her to concentrate on her research. In order to work off her excess energy, she'd scoured the bathroom and had put in a couple of loads of wash, all the while watching the clock until it was time to go over to school.

The rest of the afternoon passed with agonizing slowness. She didn't know what kind of shape Brody would be in when he finally exited those doors at three o'clock.

More nervous than she'd been after his first day at kindergarten, she went over to the school early and talked to a couple of mothers who were gathered outside the building, anxiously waiting as well.

Finally the bell rang, and the school started to empty with an explosion of shouting and giggling and chatter. Sarah held her breath and watched for her son, expecting him to be the first one out on the grass.

Once again he surprised her by not making an appearance. Ten minutes passed, and still there was no sign of him.

Worried, Sarah hurried toward the entrance, wondering what was wrong. Fearful to the point that she felt sick, she didn't see the small dynamo of energy coming out the door until it was too late and they collided.

'Brody——'

She reached out and caught him by the shoulders before he fell down. A happy face smiled up at her. The transformation was nothing short of miraculous. 'Look!' He lifted a small cage, where she could see a baby rabbit shivering. 'This is Conrad. I'm keeping him at home tonight.'

Surprised that Mrs Ruff would allow a student to take any animal home the first day of school, she said, 'Do you know how to take care of it?'

'No. But you do, don't you?'

'That's not the point,' Sarah muttered, her irritation growing. It looked as if Brody had already manipulated his teacher, who hadn't sent a note home to parents explaining anything or checked with parents to see if it was all right, let alone given instructions. 'Come inside with me, honey, and wait in the office for a minute. I want to talk to Mrs Ruff.'

'She's not my teacher.'

'What?'

'She's going to have a baby so I got another teacher.'

Probably a substitute. Everything was starting to make sense. 'Wait here and I'll be right back.'

Brody was so entranced by the rabbit, he didn't notice her departure. She didn't have the heart to take the cage from him, not quite yet, and hurried off toward the section of the building designated for the second and third graders.

Mrs Ruff's door was still open. Sarah stepped inside and noticed a set of parents at the other end of the gaily decorated room, talking quietly while they also waited for the teacher. The man's back was turned toward Sarah, but the set of his shoulders, his tall, powerful build, looked suspiciously familiar, and reminded her of someone she'd been trying without success to forget.

Her heart began to thud sickeningly. Jonah Sinclair. She'd know that well-shaped head with its dark-blond hair anywhere.

Her premonition had been correct. He and his wife had moved to Birchwood South with their child, who happened to be in the same class as Brody. She didn't think her son had realized it yet, or he would have said something when he first ran out of the building.

When Brody found out, what then? she agonized.

Hating her lack of self-control as much as her insatiable curiosity, she found herself avidly studying the face of Mrs Sinclair, a lovely young redhead who smiled up at her husband with something akin to adoration.

Sarah felt a strange twinge of pain in the region of her heart, a pain she couldn't explain or understand, and decided that now was the time to leave. The new teacher had to be somewhere else in the building. She'd ask the office to page her.

As she started out the door she heard, 'Mrs Brown? Don't go. I'd like to talk to you.' His deep voice reached out to her like a living thing and stopped her in her tracks.

On the periphery of her vision she could see the two of them walking toward her. She wanted to run away, but she knew she couldn't. Guilt and shame had a lot to answer for, and the last person in the world she wanted to meet was Mrs Sinclair.

How much had he told his wife about what had happened at Sarah's condo? Any of it? All of it? Would the other woman be understanding, and not read anything into the fact that her husband had taken off his wet clothes in a strange woman's home while they dried?

Sarah knew herself too well. No matter how much she had trusted him—and he'd never given her reason not to trust him—if Rich had come home with a story like that, she wouldn't have liked it at all.

'I'll talk to you later, when you have more time,' his wife said. She eyed Sarah coolly before she left the room, making Sarah more anxious than ever to know how much the other woman knew. The fact that he hadn't bothered to introduce them didn't appear to be a good sign, which increased her nervousness, particularly because he seemed to be in no hurry to initiate further conversation.

Out of desperation Sarah finally said, 'I had no idea you had a son or daughter going to school here. Why didn't you say something the other night?'

'If you'd shown even the slightest interest in me as a human being, I might have told you a lot of things. Not that I'm not grateful for your help,' he murmured with quiet irony. 'Why are you here? Where's Brody?'

Studying the floor, she said, 'I told him to wait in the office. Apparently Mrs Ruff has taken maternity leave and I'm not too thrilled about the person who's her temporary replacement.'

'Why is that?' he asked in a silky tone.

'Whoever she is sent Brody home with a rabbit. He's never had a pet and doesn't know the first thing about it.'

'He has to learn responsibility some time. Why not now?'

Heat suffused her face. 'The condo doesn't allow pets.'

'I doubt they'd frown on a rabbit kept overnight.'

She struggled to control her temper. 'You don't understand. The normal procedure would be to send a note home to the parents, informing us of a pet project at least a day before anything is carried out, to give us fair warning. She didn't even send instructions with it. I suppose I ought to be grateful he didn't bring home a snake.'

When he didn't say anything, a disquieting silence ensued. She had the impression he hadn't been listening to her, that his mind was on something else, just as hers was. 'Mr Sinclair—why didn't you introduce me to your wife just now?'

'Because my ex-wife lives in Hawaii.'

Sarah's head flew back and she stared at him, uncomprehending. 'But that woman you were talking to a minute ago. I—I assumed she was your wife, that you were both waiting to see the teacher.'

'No. She's the mother of one of the students.'

Quite by accident, Sarah discovered she was studying the fit of his khakis and the crew-necked sport-shirt which covered his well-defined chest.

Quickly she averted her eyes. 'I guess we've all been waiting for the new teacher. She must be very inexperienced.'

After a slight pause he said, 'Did it ever occur to you that Brody's new teacher might be a man?'

A man?

'Actually, no, but, the more I think about it, sending a rabbit home with Brody on the first day of school without first obtaining the mother's permission sounds exactly like something a man would do. A woman would know better.'

'Maybe it was an emergency measure.'

She shook her head, causing her freshly washed hair to settle around her shoulders. 'You're talking in riddles.'

He folded his arms across his chest. 'Brody was upset when he came to class this morning. He didn't want to stay.'

'How do you know that?'

'Because I'm Mrs Ruff's replacement until Christmas, when she plans to come back.'

Sarah had been prepared for any other explanation than the one he'd just given her.

'*You*?' she cried out, aghast, her thoughts reeling.

His brows furrowed. 'Why is that so incomprehensible?'

Sarah couldn't say anything for a minute. It wasn't so much that it was incomprehensible—it was *impossible*.

No wonder Brody had stayed at school today! Suddenly everything made sense. Her son had taken to Jonah Sinclair on sight and had brought his name up to Jeff several times throughout the last week. Now to have him for a teacher every day...

Brody was hungry for the kind of attention Mr Sinclair had given him at the apartment. Sarah realized her son needed a male role model, and no one could fill it better than the man standing in front of her. But he'd only be here four months. Then he'd be gone. Brody's world would collapse again. She couldn't allow that to happen. They'd been through too much.

'Look, Mr Sinclair—Brody can't stay in here.' Her voice shook. 'I'm going to transfer him to Mrs Empey's class.'

He studied her taut features for a moment. 'Your hostility toward me is no surprise. But to allow it to affect your son is unhealthy.'

'I'm not hostile toward you. I'm not anything toward you,' she blurted, if only to convince herself. 'But you're the first man Brody has responded to since my husband died. And, like him, you're not going to be around very long. I absolutely refuse to set him up for another blow.'

He rubbed his jaw. 'I'm not his father and don't share the bond your husband had with him. When I leave, he's not going to fall apart. Brody has got to learn that people will always be coming and going in his life. As long as he has you, the one sure constant, he'll be able to handle temporary relationships. It's part of growing up. A necessary part.'

She sucked in her breath, trying to make him understand. Lifting beseeching eyes to him, she said, 'I agree. In theory, everything you say makes perfect sense. But when he met you the other night, something unique happened. I can't explain it, but what Brody feels for you isn't going to go away, not if he continues to have constant contact with you.'

'It's called hero-worship,' he murmured calmly. 'I grew up without a father and went through several periods where I adored at the feet of another male who showed me some attention. The point is, I got the help I needed, then passed through those phases toward maturity without any scars.'

Fear clutched at her heart. 'I wish I could believe that where Brody is concerned. He's so different from the bright little spirit he used to be.'

'He's lost his confidence.'

She bowed her head. 'I know.'

'Has he told you the reason why he hates school so much?'

She shook her head. 'No. He doesn't say anything to me except that he doesn't want to go.'

'That's because he needs you to be proud of him and doesn't want you to know what's going on.'

Reluctantly, her gaze swerved to his. She was almost afraid to hear. 'What *is* going on?'

'We had lunch together, and while he devoured one of my peanut butter sandwiches he told me that all his friends are taller than he is. That's why no one ever chooses him to be on their team at recess. He hates being called "shrimp" and "shorty".'

She swallowed hard. 'The other day he mentioned something about his dad being short, but I had no idea he was getting made fun of.'

'Right now that's an issue with him, which is why he admires me. So I told him a story about what it was like to be the tallest boy in school, who was so skinny everyone called me "string-bean" and "Olive Oyl".'

Sarah's lips quivered in spite of the gravity of the situation. She tried to imagine him at that stage of life, and couldn't. 'I don't believe it.'

His quick smile made her heart turn over. 'Your son said the same thing, so I told him I'd bring a picture tomorrow and let him judge for himself. In the meantime, I picked him to be captain today and let him choose his own soccer team for recess. He can outrun most everyone in the class. Next week we'll be holding foot races and I fully expect he'll win some of them.'

Since before Rich's death, this had probably been the happiest day of Brody's life. 'I wonder why he didn't tell me you were the teacher when I bumped into him in front of the school earlier?'

'I asked him not to say anything until I'd had a chance to phone you at home this evening.'

'Why?'

'Surely you don't need to ask me that question?' his voice grated. 'You didn't like me the second you laid eyes on me the other night, and he's fully aware of it. I didn't want you to transfer him to another class without first giving me an opportunity to hear your reasons. Now is as good a time as any.'

Adrenaline surged through her body and she felt warm all over. 'I—I don't dislike you. If I gave you that impression, I didn't mean to.'

'As I recall, you couldn't get rid of me fast enough, which is hardly flattering considering the fact that Brody tells me men are constantly coming and going from your condo, often staying for hours. I know that's true because the other night, when my taxi pulled up in front, I saw one of them leave your condo and drive off in the rain.'

Hot-faced, she declared, 'I'm a legal researcher and work out of my home as much as possible so I won't be away from Brody.'

'If that's the case, then why do you feel threatened by me?'

She lifted her slightly rounded chin. 'You don't threaten me, Mr Sinclair.'

'I'm glad to hear it. Then I take it you don't mind that your son nominated you to be a room mother? As you know, there are dozens of activities throughout the year where parental help is necessary. The first will be the eye-screening examinations at the end of the month. But if you can't fit that into your busy schedule——'

'I'll make the time, Mr Sinclair,' she declared abruptly. 'Brody will always be my first priority.'

'Does that mean you'll let him keep the rabbit overnight? When he was so upset about coming to school, I told him Conrad was scared because it was his first day, too, and he needed a friend. Hopefully, in the morning, Brody will be so anxious to show me he's taken good care of the rabbit that he'll forget to remember that he hates school.'

Sarah eyed him covertly. Not only was he an amazing teacher, he was a first-rate psychologist. But in Brody's case he didn't need a rabbit to bring him back to school tomorrow.

Something—someone—far more compelling had power over her son. Someone who knew how to reach him every bit as profoundly as his own father, maybe even more so. Jonah Sinclair terrified Sarah.

CHAPTER THREE

'Mom?'

Sarah whirled around to see her son standing in the doorway carrying the rabbit cage, his deep-set blue eyes guarded as he eyed the two of them.

'Brody, honey——' The events of the last little while had made her forget everything, including her son, who'd been forced to wait in the office far too long.

'Are you mad 'cause I didn't tell you about Jonah?'

Right now Sarah could have wished for an olive complexion, instead of one that her father used to tell her reminded him of rare porcelain. Since meeting Jonah Sinclair, she was constantly feeling hot and prickly, and it showed.

'No, of course not.' Which was the truth, but she'd have given anything if the two of them had never met.

Maybe it was hero-worship on Brody's part, but the more she was getting to know Jonah Sinclair, the more she was convinced that Brody wouldn't get over the loss once Mrs Ruff came back. Sarah dreaded to think what life would be like at that point, but what could she do? Brody had already bonded to him.

'Brody, I think if he's going to be your teacher, you should call him Mr Sinclair.'

'It's all right,' Jonah assured her. 'Mr Sinclair is too formal. I've encouraged everyone to call me Jonah, and would appreciate it if you would, too.'

A shiver passed through her body. Everything he said and did unsettled Sarah, so that she felt flustered and out of sorts.

'Do you want to see where I sit?'

'I—I was just about to ask you to show me. Why don't you put the cage on one of the desks for a minute, to give the rabbit a rest?'

'Okay.'

She followed Brody down the second aisle to the third seat, all the while aware of Jonah's gaze on her long, slender legs. She was glad she'd worn a tailored blouse and skirt. Her heart still raced with suffocating speed whenever she remembered the night he'd seen her in that wisp of a nightgown. The look in his eyes had melted her bones, making her lethargic and breathless. If the truth was known, she was feeling that way right now, and couldn't seem to do anything about it.

'Where does Jeff sit?' she asked, trying to ignore the feelings Brody's teacher had unwittingly aroused in her. Much as she hated to admit it, Rich had never had this effect on her. He'd been a tender, considerate lover, but he'd never made her feel this shaken, never made her ache with longings totally foreign to her. It had to stop! She had to make it stop!

'On the other side of the room.'

At the sound of Brody's voice, Sarah blinked. She'd been so engrossed in forbidden thoughts she'd forgotten that her son was telling her about the seating arrangements.

His calm response puzzled her. She had thought, of course, he'd be in hysterics at having to be separated from Jeff. Without conscious thought, her eyes sought Jonah's.

'There are several new students who've just moved into Birchwood,' he murmured by way of explanation. 'Brody and Jeff are old-timers and can show them around.'

Another master-stroke. Jonah knew instinctively what to do.

And Sarah knew what she had to do.

'We'd better be getting home, Brody. I'm sure your teacher has a lot of work to finish up, and that rabbit is probably hungry and thirsty. I've got some salad in the fridge he'll like.'

'Okay, Mom. See you tomorrow, Jonah.'

Jonah nodded, then switched his gaze to Sarah, watching her through shuttered eyes. 'In a few days you'll be getting a note about a field trip we're taking to the local fire station. The days of the eye-screening will be listed as well. I'm going to need help with both.'

'You'll do it, won't you, Mom?' Brody pleaded, with a hint of anxiety in his voice.

He had no idea what he was asking. 'Yes, honey. I've already told Jonah I would.'

A smile of relief broke out on his gamin face, whose features reminded her so much of Rich, and a fresh stab of guilt consumed her. For the last half-hour she'd been comparing her feelings for her husband to those for Jonah Sinclair, a near stranger who had done nothing overt to make her think he was interested in her.

How could she betray Rich like that? How could she even be thinking of another man?

She glanced at her wedding-ring. When they'd said their vows, she'd made a secret vow in her heart never to remove it.

Filled with remorse, she promised herself that from here on out she'd stay emotionally detached from Brody's teacher. Four months would pass soon enough, and the only times she'd have to see him would be when the entire class was around.

Without a backward glance she ushered Brody from the room, unaware she'd been holding her breath until they'd reached the outside of the school, where she drank in gulps of hot air. Since the storm, the temperature had soared once more, making it the hottest September second on record. The elements seemed to be keeping pace with her sizzling emotions.

Fortunately Brody was so preoccupied with the rabbit he didn't seem to notice Sarah's silence. The rest of the afternoon and evening passed in a whirl of activity as they ate dinner and watched the rabbit chomp on lettuce and carrots, sending them both into bursts of laughter at his antics.

For the first time since she could remember, Brody didn't fight her when she told him it was time to go to bed. They put the rabbit on the night-stand next to his pillow. When Brody said his prayers, he asked God to bless his teacher and the rabbit, and his mother, of course. Before he went to sleep, he told Sarah he couldn't wait to go to school the next day.

For the rest of the week he was a model child. Sarah should have been grateful for the change in her son. Instead, she cried herself to sleep every night, because she knew Brody was riding for a fall.

She didn't feel the slightest bit thankful that Jonah Sinclair had chosen teaching as a career, and couldn't understand why he had come to Colorado. Every day she grew more alarmed as her son came home from school singing his praises. It was Jonah this and Jonah that. Jonah was awesome, according to Brody, who couldn't wait until Sarah went on the bus with them to the fire station.

According to her son, Talia's mother would be accompanying them too, which was a great relief to Sarah. She'd have another adult to talk to besides Jonah and could keep the field trip on a strictly professional basis.

But, as it turned out, the other room mother happened to be the redheaded woman Sarah had seen in the classroom on the first day of school. Sarah needn't have worried that she might have to deal on a one-to-one basis with Jonah.

Other than an impersonal glance and nod at Sarah, when he introduced her and Lynette to each other, Jonah seemed to go out of his way to ignore her. *En route* he sat up by the driver and spent the bulk of time talking to Talia's mother, who ignored Sarah as if she weren't there.

Once they reached the fire station, the two of them disappeared, leaving Sarah to manage the entire group of students as best she could while the fire chief talked to the kids.

What irritated her most was that Jonah apparently didn't notice or care. When the tour of the building began, Sarah found herself alone with the kids as they were shown the various rooms. She didn't see Jonah again until they ended up in the bay where the engines were kept.

When the fire chief asked who was going to ride in the big truck while they backed it out to be washed and serviced, every hand went up, but it was Jonah who broke away from the other woman and made the decision.

To her astonishment, he singled out Brody, who cried 'Yippee!' While the other children expressed their disappointment, he scrambled to the fire chief's side where he was given a helmet to wear before being hoisted into the seat next to one of the firefighters.

Sarah could only imagine the thrill this was for Brody, and wouldn't have taken the moment away from him for anything. But, as the bay doors opened, she heard several of the kids complaining that Brody was the teacher's pet. She was sure they'd spoken loudly enough for Sarah to hear on purpose, because they kept turning around and looking at her.

Naturally only one of the students would have been chosen to ride up-front, but if since the beginning of school Jonah had been showing this kind of favoritism to her son, she could understand why the other kids would resent it.

Hadn't Jonah told Sarah that he'd made Brody a captain at recess on the first day of school? Had any of the other kids been given a rabbit to take home all week?

The incident marred the outing for her, reinforcing her fear that Jonah's attention to Brody was out of the ordinary, the very situation she'd hoped to avoid.

She decided to broach the subject with Jonah, but never got a chance because Lynette monopolized him, forcing Sarah to sit near the rear of the bus. The fact that he allowed the other woman such exclusivity led Sarah to wonder if they didn't have a relationship outside of school. Not that she cared.

Her only concern was Brody and his expectations. When Jonah could no longer meet them, Sarah would be the one left to pick up the pieces. More than ever she needed to tell him to stop singling out Brody, stop giving him special treatment.

Maybe the best way to handle it would be to write him a note and send it to school through the mail, thus avoiding a confrontation.

On the following Saturday, she sat down at the dining-table to compose the short letter, choosing her words carefully. While she was deep in thought, Jeff and another friend, Kevin, came over to the house to play with Brody. At noon they decided to go to Jeff's.

By then Sarah had finished the note and decided to mail it on her way to the courthouse. She told Brody she'd pick him up from Jeff's at two, then they'd go do a little more school shopping. He needed another pair of pants and some underwear.

But, later in the day, when she'd done her errands in town and had driven to Jeff's condo, Jeff and Kevin came running out to the car to tell her Brody had gone home a long time ago because he didn't feel very good.

Alarmed, because he'd left Jeff's without permission and would be locked out, Sarah hurried to the house, but Brody was nowhere in sight. Her neighbors, a retired couple living in the condo attached to theirs, said they hadn't seen him.

With a pit in her stomach, she started driving around the complex, hoping to spot him. She deliberately cruised by the clubhouse, which had been kept open because of the unseasonably hot weather, hoping one of the kids hanging around the pool area might have seen him.

As she slowed down to call a couple of them over to the car she heard, as clear as a bell above the laughter and splashing, 'Jonah—— Here I go again. Catch me!'

Drawn to the sound of Brody's voice, she caught a brief glimpse of his wet head before he jumped off the high dive.

An anger she'd never known before charged her body with adrenaline.

The boy who didn't want to swim anymore, the boy who refused to take swimming lessons, was cavorting in the pool with Jonah Sinclair and having the time of his life.

Brody had lied to her and to his friends, all so he could be with the one man whom she, at this point, wished on the other side of the planet.

Jonah was even more to blame than Brody, because he was the adult and knew better. From the first day of their meeting in the classroom, he had known *exactly* how Sarah felt about her son spending any time with him outside of school. She'd tried to explain what a vulnerable time this was for Brody, but he'd obviously dismissed her fears as so much nonsense and intended to carry on as he saw fit.

She didn't remember pulling her car into an empty parking space, or walking through the clubhouse to the pool. Picking her way past the lifeguard, she ignored the various people enjoying the open plunge because her eyes were riveted on the charismatic male at the deep end of the pool, encouraging one young, dark-headed boy to do the backstroke.

The fact that he lay flat in the water and did everything Jonah said without any qualms showed the enormous amount of trust her son had placed in this man who'd so recently arrived on their doorstep in a rainstorm.

Shaking with suppressed fury, she walked over to the ladder. 'Brody? It's time to get out of the pool!' she called to him, but was afraid he couldn't hear her. His eyes were tightly closed while he rotated his arms to reach the opposite side. He had no idea she was there.

Still supporting Brody under his back, Jonah turned his head, and their gazes met head-on. Hers was a burning blue, and for once she didn't avoid him. 'Please inform my son that I'm waiting for him in the car outside the clubhouse.'

He studied her set features, the way the hot breeze outlined the mold of her body and legs, before he said in a level tone, 'Why don't you come in? Brody's been practicing for you.'

His utter disregard for her wishes, his audacious perusal which made her tremble, fed her anger as much as his hard good looks and fit body. In the sunlight, with his dark-blond hair slicked back like a pagan Apollo, no man in the pool or anywhere else could compare to him.

'Tell Brody I expect to see him outside within two minutes.'

Turning swiftly on her heel, she walked away, feeling his veiled eyes on her retreating back. Much as she'd wanted to lash out at him, she was afraid that if she'd stayed there another second she might have said something in front of an entire pool full of people that she'd regret later on.

Until she reached the car, she had no idea that Jonah had followed her. 'Not so fast, Mrs Brown,' he muttered, in a voice of quiet contempt. 'I'd like a word with you.'

Sarah whirled around, her temper flaring, causing her glistening black hair to swirl against her flushed cheeks.

'Not as much as I would have liked one with you the other day, but, as you were otherwise occupied with Talia's mother, I had to resort to writing you a letter, which you'll receive on Monday.'

'I'm here now,' he muttered icily, and grabbed hold of her arm before she could get in the car. His grip was firm, but if she tried to pull away from him, she had an idea she would know its full power. 'You've been sending out signals explosive enough to set off an atomic bomb. What in the hell is wrong with you, lady?'

'*You* are what's wrong,' she fired back hotly.

His mouth became a taut line of anger. 'Do you hate all men, or just me in particular?'

'I hate what you're doing to a vulnerable, fatherless boy, who's as fragile as glass right now.'

His mouth held a sardonic twist. 'What's the matter?' he murmured unpleasantly. 'Do you intend to make Brody wallow for years on end in your morbid widow's grief? He's a normal, loving boy, full of zest and vigor, who's going to end up dysfunctional if you don't wake up and pull yourself out of the morass of self-pity you've created.'

'*How dare you*?'

'Oh, I dare, lady,' he ground out. 'I haven't even started.'

'That's what *you* think.'

She jerked her arm away and got in the car, slamming the door hard, and not a minute too soon, because Brody suddenly emerged from the clubhouse.

He hesitated when he saw the two of them together. No doubt he could feel the hostility.

'Mom?' he said tentatively.

'Get in the car, Brody.'

He hurried to do her bidding and ran past Jonah without saying anything. The striped bathing suit he carried in his hand was proof that he'd planned this outing with Jonah ahead of time and had worn it under his shorts when he'd left for Jeff's.

His wet dark hair and face couldn't disguise the fact that he'd been crying.

'I'm s-sorry Mom,' his voice croaked as he got in the front seat and shut the door.

'I am too,' she muttered, backing out of the parking space in a jerky motion. Through the rearview mirror she could see Jonah—still in his swimming trunks—watching her with an expression of distaste on his features.

She could have cared less, and readjusted the mirror so she didn't have to put up with his condemning stare. Once she'd cleared the area, she took off in the opposite direction, taut with rage that he could dare make a judgement when he knew nothing about what was going on inside her. *Nothing*.

After they'd been driving for a minute, she said in a terse voice, 'Why didn't you tell me that you were going to meet Jonah today?'

Brody was crying in earnest now. 'B-Because I knew you'd say no if you found out.'

She swung into the carport of her condo too sharply and had to slam on the brakes. 'You're right about that. He's your teacher! Remember your kindergarten and first-grade teachers? You didn't spend time with them outside of school. Mr Sinclair is a busy man with a lot of responsibility. He has a right to his privacy.'

'He said he l-liked having me around,' Brody hiccuped.

'I'm sure he likes all his students, but bothering him while he's swimming or playing tennis or anything else is wrong.' She flicked a glance at his downbent head. 'What's our rule about the pool?'

'That I never go unless you know about it. But Jonah was there——'

Her eyes closed tightly. 'How can I trust you anymore, Brody? How do you think I felt when I heard you'd gone home from Jeff's and I couldn't find you?'

He sobbed quietly. 'Bad.'

'If I ever find out that you've lied again, or bothered him one more time, I'm going to put you in a different school. As it is, I'm planning to speak to Mrs Empey about transferring you to her class on Monday.'

'*No*!' he cried out hysterically. 'No, Mom. Don't take me out of Jonah's class. I promise I won't do it again. I promise.'

His reaction shook her to the depths. She'd never seen him like this, not even after Rich had died.

'I was going to take you shopping, but I've changed my mind. Come in the house and get your shower.'

She got out of the car and opened the back door of the condo.

'A-Are you going to move me out of Jonah's class?' he asked in a panic-stricken voice, after they'd gone into the kitchen.

'I'm seriously thinking about it. You never used to lie to me when——' she broke off talking before she said something else she'd regret. Sarah felt like a monster, but she was fast losing control of an impossible situation. 'How would you like it if I told you one thing and did another? What if you couldn't trust me?'

But she might as well have saved her breath because he only cried harder. 'You won't take me away from Jonah, will you? I promise to be good.'

'Oh, Brody.' She shook her head and the tears started. 'I'm not trying to hurt you, honey.' She reached out and crushed him in her arms, rocking him back and forth. I'm trying to save you from being hurt again, but I'm afraid it's already too late.

'I love Jonah, Mom. Please let me stay in his class.'

Sarah shuddered in pain. It *was* too late.

'All right,' she finally whispered, 'but only on one condition. That you obey the rules, or that's it.'

'I promise!' He gave a great shout of happiness, then dashed out of the kitchen to take his shower.

Sarah only made it as far as the couch in the living-room before she collapsed in despair. The confrontation with Jonah had turned her world upside-down. The words he'd thrown at her made her sound so ugly and sick.

Did he honestly see her that way? A grieving widow *wallowing* in her pain? Did other people have that same impression, that she was turning Brody into a neurotic basket-case because of her morbid behavior, as Jonah had called it? She could hardly bear it.

'Mom?' he said a few minutes later, all fresh and clean. 'Why are you still crying?'

She jumped up from the couch and wiped her eyes. 'I'm just being a mom. When I couldn't find you, I got scared because I thought you were really sick and wouldn't be able to get in the house. Which reminds me that we should give a key to the people next door, in case you should ever get locked out by accident.'

'I'm sorry I went to the pool without telling you. I won't do it again.'

She sniffed and smoothed the hair off her cheeks. 'Let's forget about it and go get a hamburger. Then we'll finish your school shopping.'

His eyes lit up. 'I thought you changed your mind.'

'I did. But I've changed it again. I love you, Brody. More than you'll ever know. I don't want us to have any trouble.'

'I love you, too, Mom.' He flung his arms around her.

She clung to him, praying it wasn't too late to undo any damage she might have unwittingly inflicted.

CHAPTER FOUR

THE following week passed by with no incidents to speak of. Brody was careful not to talk too much about Jonah and their household seemed to be getting back to some kind of normalcy.

When the weekend came, Brody, along with a couple of boys from school, had gone over to Jeff's for his first sleepover.

Sarah decided to take advantage of her free evening—the first one she'd had in months—and phone Sylvia Barrett. It was time to start making plans for the Christmas holidays.

Sylvia's husband had died along with Rich in the coast guard accident. For months afterward they'd consoled each other, and had become good friends, deciding to make a tradition of spending Christmas Eve and Christmas with each other. They both felt it was the best way to honor their husbands and keep the children's memories of them alive.

Sarah and Brody had gone to San Diego last Christmas Eve. This year it was Sylvia's turn to come to Denver with her two daughters, Nancy and Susan, aged eight and five. The condo had a guest-room and there was a hide-a-bed in the study to accommodate everyone.

But, before she placed the call, Sarah had to finish cleaning Brody's room and put his sheets in the wash.

'I don't believe it!' she cried out a few minutes later, when she heard water spilling over the top of the washing-machine. It proceeded to run down the sides and slowly spread across the laundry-room floor. Before long it would ruin the new linoleum Valerie had put down in the kitchen before they'd left for the Far East.

Obviously the timer had gone haywire and the filling cycle hadn't shut off. Standing with bare feet in cold water, Sarah quickly searched for the taps. The hot tap worked easily enough, but the cold water tap refused to turn, no matter how much pressure she applied.

Where was the water turn-off? Hal had mentioned it, but she couldn't remember.

With no time to lose, she raced out the back door to the neighbors. They were usually home. But, after repeatedly ringing the door bell and knocking hard, she realized they must be out.

She had no choice but to run along the access drive to the next group of townhouses. While she waited for someone to answer the first door she came to, her eyes strayed to a hunter-green Jaguar parked in the stall. She hadn't lived in the complex long enough to know many of her neighbors and hoped it was a man who owned that car, someone who possessed brute strength in case it was needed.

She thought she heard a noise coming from within and knocked frantically, praying for a response. To her relief, a light finally went on and the door opened. A tall, muscular male stood in the aperture... Maybe she was hallucinating. But when she opened her eyes again, he was still there.

She let out a gasp. *Jonah*——

She hadn't seen him since that ghastly incident at the pool, and had been dreading having to face him on the first of the month when she went to school to help with the eye-screening tests.

How long had he lived here? Was this another secret Brody had been keeping from her?

'If you're looking for your son, he's not here,' his voice grated. 'Before you accuse me of any more sins, you should know that he has never been invited inside this condo, let alone been encouraged to visit.' The words dropped like rocks. He'd read her mind with uncanny perception and it brought the blood coursing to her cheeks.

'I—I didn't come to——' she started to explain, but couldn't go on, not when his scathing look almost paralyzed her. 'N-Never mind,' she whispered in a defeated voice. The flood in her sister's townhouse didn't leave her time to dwell on the precariousness of their relationship. Maybe someone living in the condos on the other side of her sister's would be home and could help her.

'Where in the hell do you think you're going?'

In a lightning move his hand snaked out and grabbed her wrist before she could get away, holding her fast.

'If you didn't come for Brody, then why are you here? Answer me!' he demanded. 'There has to be a reason, because I happen to know you wouldn't come within ten miles of me if you could possibly help it,' he bit out.

'Please, let me go——' she cried in panic, as much from the physical contact, which made her body burn, as from the potential disaster at home. 'There's a flood in my condo. I couldn't find the water turn-off and water is pouring into the kitchen from the washing-machine. My brother-in-law will kill me if the new linoleum is destroyed.'

'A flood——' he muttered beneath his breath, his expression incredulous as he finally released his hold on her arm.

Galvanized into action by the alarm in her voice, he called to some people in the background that there was a problem.

Sarah was mortified that he had company, because they'd probably heard the vitriol in Jonah's voice. She watched helplessly as three men followed him out the door. With the grace of a panther, he disappeared down the drive.

When she caught up with them, they were already inside her townhouse, dwarfing the kitchen. To her dismay she could see water pooling under the dinette set.

Everything happened in a kind of daze as one of the men grabbed a broom and started sweeping water out the back door while Jonah disappeared into the laundry-room and found the turn-off behind the dryer.

Sarah smoothed a shoulder-length tendril of dark hair behind her ear and sighed in relief when the water stopped.

'Thank heavens you were home,' she cried in gratitude, lifting her eyes to his probing gaze, a look which was coolly assessing and seemed to be asking a question.

'Give us some towels and we'll dry your floor.'

She shook her head, unwilling to be any more in debt to him, especially when there was such enmity between them. Aside from everything else, she couldn't handle his male presence, which was far too disturbing to her senses.

'You've saved the kitchen and my sanity. I wouldn't dream of asking you to clean up. I can't thank you enough for what you did. All of you,' she added lamely when she realized she'd forgotten about his friends, standing around smiling at her with open male interest.

Her T-shirt and shorts were adequate, the kind of thing she slipped into at home after-hours in the heat of summer, but not the type of attire she'd have worn in front of company.

'We were glad to assist,' Jonah murmured, before introducing them to Sarah. The whole time he spoke, he was studying the classic lines of her oval face through narrowed lids. The enigmatic expression lurking in his eyes revealed nothing of his inner feelings.

Perhaps they sensed the tension between her and Jonah, because one by one the men said goodnight and left. She expected Jonah to follow them out the door, but he stayed planted to the spot, with his hands on his hips. His demeanor sent a frisson of apprehension through her trembling body.

'How long have you known I've lived there?'

His question brought her up short, making her feel unstrung and on the defensive. 'I knew nothing until you opened the door,' she said frostily.

By his silence, she surmised that he patently didn't believe her.

'I've only been in Colorado since June, when we came to house-sit my sister's place while she and her husband are in the Orient. Except for the people next door, and a few of Brody's friends, I haven't a clue who lives in the complex.'

When he still said nothing she added, 'I'm sorry to have interrupted your party.'

An eyebrow quirked. 'It was hardly a party. I was having a meeting with some of my staff.'

Sarah blinked. 'Staff? I—I don't understand. You're a teacher.'

'For the moment I am.'

Her head came up and she stared at him in utter confusion. 'I don't understand.'

'My life's work is tied up in a software company I started years ago in California. We create and manufacture programs of all kinds, for use in both the government and public domain.'

Quickly Sarah's mind grappled with the new revelation. Without thinking, she blurted, 'You're not the Sinclair of Sinclair Techtronics, are you?'

His face remained impassive. 'Guilty as charged.'

In a flash, everything started to fit. A year ago she remembered being in one of the attorneys' offices in San Diego and reading an article on Jonah's company in *Forbes* magazine. The young tycoon who'd started a business in his basement had risen to dizzying heights which spanned a mere decade, accomplishing more than most men hoped to accomplish over a lifetime.

The power and charisma that held the children at Birchwood Elementary in thrall was no longer a mystery. Though Brody had no idea what kind of man was teaching his class, he had instinctively responded to Jonah's dynamism and that aura of confidence and strength which had captured the attention of the corporate world.

Swallowing hard, she said, 'What on earth are you doing teaching Brody's second-grade class?' The man was worth millions—could buy his own island or mountain, live wherever he wanted.

'I needed a living laboratory to try out a new product I've developed as an educational tool to teach whole language skills to elementary students. Before I can sell it on the market, I have to have hands-on experience and test it, work out the bugs. A friend of mine moved here a few years ago and is now superintendent of your school district. He worked out an arrangement with Mrs Ruff.'

Sarah stared at him in astonishment. '*That's* why you're teaching Brody's class?' Her thoughts were flying hither and yon. 'Have you ever taught elementary school before?'

'No,' he answered with bald honesty, a characteristic she was forced to admire, but only with the greatest of reluctance. 'She coaches me over the telephone. Most days I'm not even one step ahead. I'm afraid my teaching experience lies more in a few guest lecture spots at MIT and Princeton.'

A long silence ensued while she tried to absorb everything. 'You're a born teacher,' she said, before she realized it had slipped out.

Something in his eyes quickened. 'That must have cost you a great deal to admit. If the truth were known, I'm surprised how much I'm enjoying it.' His forceful gaze trapped hers. 'Needless to say, I'd be run out of town on a rail if the parents knew I lacked the conventional qualifications.'

As far as Sarah was concerned, Jonah Sinclair's success with Brody could garner him the Teacher of the Year award, but she kept that opinion to herself. 'If parents knew who you were, you'd be zeroed in on by the media and would never be able to call your life your own again.'

'That would be one way of getting rid of me sooner,' he said, with undisguised disdain. 'You'd better seize the opportunity while you can. No telling how much more damage I'll inflict on the Brown family before my four months are up.'

Sarah struggled for composure, stung by his derisive remarks and oddly troubled by the strange sense of loss she felt because he'd be leaving at Christmas. It didn't make any sense.

The negative tension surrounding them became almost tangible. 'For the record, I had planned to rent the *other* Mrs Brown's condo while she vacationed in Florida with her family. But she passed away unexpectedly and word didn't reach my realtor in time, which was why there was no answer that night.'

She took a deep breath. 'You don't owe me an explanation.'

'You're going to get one anyway,' he came back abruptly. 'There were no other townhouses to rent. The condo I'm in now was the only one for sale, so I grabbed it. Knowing how much it would displease you to find out I lived this close to you, I chose not to say anything and hoped you would never find out.'

'Jonah——' she spread her hands in frustration '—I...'

'Brody knows where I live,' he continued on, oblivious to her reaction. 'But, sensing your resentment toward me, he hasn't said anything to you. Rest assured he'll never step foot inside my condo, certainly not without your express permission, and we both know that will never happen.'

'I—I've told you, I have nothing personal against you. It's Brody I'm concerned about.'

'Where is he?'

'At a sleepover. Jeff's father is setting up tents on their front lawn.'

'Considering your fear that Brody will develop too strong an attachment to a man other than his father, I'm surprised you would allow him to be around Jeff's father.'

She bit her lip, determined not to rise to the bait. 'Whether you know it or not, he needs a break from you.'

His observation cut like a knife. 'You're over-stepping your bounds, Mr Sinclair,' she said icily.

'If I am, it's because your son is struggling with a problem that only you have the power to solve, but you're too blind to recognize it.'

'Now wait just a minute!' she called to him when he started to walk out the kitchen door.

'I don't have a minute. I was in the middle of a conference and need to get back to it.'

Her chest heaved in growing panic and anger. 'How late will it last?'

He shrugged his shoulders negligently. 'Another hour. Maybe more. Why the interest?'

Her eyes were hot blue flames of indignation. 'You *know* why.'

After a long pause he asked, 'What are your plans for this evening?'

'I—I'm staying in.' She wasn't about to tell him anything else.

His expression was indecipherable. 'In the circumstances, that's probably a wise decision.'

He wasn't about to make this easy, damn him. 'I have no idea what you're getting at. Shall I come over there?'

'I think for Brody's sake I'd better come here.'

'What are you talking about?'

'Before too long he'll probably be calling you to pick him up and take him home.'

Sarah frowned. 'Why would he do that?'

'I don't have time to go into it. Expect me around nine-thirty. I'll bring my wrench and see if I can't close that tap, otherwise you'll be without water until you can get a plumber over here.'

Sarah watched helplessly as he walked out the back door. She felt like throwing something at him, or shaking him so he'd tell her what was going on with Brody. But she couldn't, not when he was holding an important business meeting with the men who worked for him. She was still trying to grasp the fact that Jonah had come from a world most people only dreamed about, a world she couldn't relate to.

Thanks to Jonah, she couldn't possibly concentrate on anything else tonight, let alone call Sylvia. With sinking heart, Sarah realized she needed to get to the bottom of this latest crisis of Brody's, whatever it was.

The floor still felt wet beneath her bare feet, reminding her that what had started out as a minor crisis when the washer wouldn't shut off had turned into something much more volatile.

Jonah was angry.

After the way she'd warned him off Brody, she supposed he had every right to be. But she hadn't been prepared for the dark, ominous quality about him that made her feel small and uncomfortable. And devastated.

On a shaky breath, she shut the door and hurried down the hall to the linen-closet. With towels in hand, she went to work on the kitchen floor, plagued with Jonah's image and the innuendoes he'd tossed her way, which had been meant to prick. Little did he know they'd done real damage.

Yet an inner voice whispered that if it hadn't been for him, she might have had a real disaster on her hands. To think he'd been living so close to her for who knew how long, and Brody had never said a word!

She worked harder and faster, but getting the floor dry turned out to be a bigger project than she had anticipated. By the time she'd finished getting up all the moisture and had changed clothes, she heard a knock on the back door and knew it had to be Jonah.

Straightening her navy cotton sweater over the hips of her white skirt, she hurried to the kitchen, anxious to get this over with.

When she opened the door to him she discovered he'd changed into less formal clothes, and was wearing a well-worn T-shirt and shorts that rode low on his hips. Her eyes traveled to his muscular thighs and hair-roughened legs.

She felt a curling warmth travel through her body to its core. Worse, her mouth had gone so dry she couldn't make a sound. But, if she was reading the situation correctly, his judgemental eyes swept over her, then dismissed her as if he found her wanting.

'I'll tackle the tap first.' His tone was civil enough, but there was something intangible and aloof in the way he spoke that told her he didn't like this situation any more than she did.

In an economy of movement, he stepped into the laundry-room and moved the dryer so he could get behind it. Sarah marveled at the adept way he used the wrench to make the cold water tap turn and found herself watching the play of muscles across his back.

'It's closed now, but you'll need a plumber to bring a new part and install it. I'll turn your water on.'

Too soon he had everything in working order and put back in place.

'Thank you,' she whispered as he turned around, catching her staring at him.

Without saying a word, he moved swiftly to the kitchen sink and washed his hands. Over his broad shoulder he said, 'After we've had our talk, you may wish you'd reserved your thanks.'

She tried to quell the hammering of her heart, brought on not only by his nearness, but also by the prospect of the unpleasant news he had to tell her about Brody. 'Is it that bad?'

He dried his hands and turned to her, leaning one hip against the counter. Flashing her an impenetrable glance, he murmured, 'That all depends on how you handle it.'

'Are you purposely trying to hurt me?' she demanded, driven to the edge.

'No,' came the low reply.

'Don't you know Brody means more to me than life itself?'

'*Does* he?'

On a strangled sob she cried, 'How can you stand there and ask me a question like that?'

'I can because Brody doesn't think you love him anymore.'

'*What*?' The pain was too much.

'He hears you crying at night.'

Sarah looked away, embarrassed to think this man was privy to something so personal and intimate.

'Have you ever told him *why* you cry?'

'Of course not,' she murmured. 'I've tried to hide it from him.'

'The walls in these condos are thin.'

'I think you've said enough.'

'I haven't even started. What are the tears about?'

She stiffened. 'That's none of your business.'

'I'm afraid Brody has made it my business. He says his grandparents have never wanted to see him, and he thinks you wish he was dead now that your husband has passed away.'

His words tore her apart. 'He actually told you that?' Her agony was so great, she held on to the chair-back for support.

'If you don't believe me, ask him,' he said in a solemn voice. 'He needs an opportunity to find out what's going on inside of you, but all you've shown him is tears. He has no way to deal with them. To a child, there's nothing more daunting than a parent who cries all the time.'

'Since when did you become the expert?' She lashed out in her pain.

'My mother remarried, but it didn't work out. When he left, she never stopped crying. I thought she missed him so much that she couldn't love me anymore. I didn't learn the truth until several years later, when a great deal of damage had already been done to my psyche.' A bleakness entered his eyes, wounding her. 'Apparently he'd left her pregnant, with a string of debts. Her distress brought on a miscarriage.'

Sarah shuddered. 'How horrible.'

He nodded soberly. 'It was. The irony being that she loved me so much, she worked herself into an early grave to support me. A few words of explanation would have made all the difference in my life.'

His words were so heartbreaking, Sarah couldn't speak.

'I think I know how Brody's mind is working these days. He can never be completely carefree because there's always that fear lurking deep inside him.'

'Wh-What fear?'

'That one day you'll abandon him.'

She put a hand to her throat, shattered by Jonah's insight.

'Mark my words. He'll never last the whole night at the sleepover, for fear you'll be gone when he gets back.'

Sarah couldn't take any more. She buried her face in her hands and sobbed, terrified he was right. That was why Brody had clung to her all summer, why he'd turned to Jonah, whose own tragic experience early in life had made him sensitive to Brody's insecurity.

Jonah's phenomenal success in business had most likely come as a result of the refiner's fire, but there'd been pain. She'd heard it in his voice, and didn't want that for her son.

'Brody——' She cried his name, her shoulders shaking, but the timing couldn't have been worse, because there was a knock at the front door and then the buzzer sounded repeatedly.

'Mom?' came a frantic-sounding young voice. 'Mom—it's me! Let me in!'

In a state of shock, she lifted tear-drenched eyes to Jonah.

His flashed fire. 'For the love of heaven, don't just stand there!' The veins stood out in his neck.

'While I handle him, go fix your face and put on those shorts you were wearing earlier,' he ordered, in a commanding voice that brooked no argument.

'My shorts?' she said on a gasp.

'No questions. Just do it,' he ground out.

From the fierce look he darted her, this was one time when she had no choice but to follow his lead, because Brody was the important one here.

'I'll hurry,' she murmured, and flew out of the kitchen toward the bedroom, changing into the same clothes she'd had on earlier.

She could hear voices coming from the kitchen, which meant Jonah was detaining him. Luckily Brody didn't run into the bathroom until after she'd washed her face and was applying lotion.

'Mom——' He threw his arms around her hips and squeezed her. 'Jonah says you're going to bring a tent and come to the sleepover with us.'

Her hands stilled on her face. Through her long lashes, she could see the stars in Brody's eyes.

Jonah. Jonah. What have you done?

She leaned over and cupped her son's face in her hands. 'Don't you think your friends will get mad if I show up at your party?'

'Heck, no. Jeff's dad brought me home and he wants you and Jonah to come. Jonah'll be back in a minute. He went to get his tent and sleeping-bag, because he knows we don't have any of that kind of stuff.'

At the thought of sleeping anywhere near Jonah Sinclair, an unbidden thrill of excitement charged her body.

As if he were possessed of hidden knowledge not given to other mortals, Jonah had turned a potentially destructive situation into an opportunity for her to reinforce her love for her son.

Rich had never taken them camping. He had spent so much time at sea that when he did come home, he liked to stay put. The idea of sleeping out under the stars on the neighbor's lawn held tremendous appeal for Sarah. She didn't have to look at Brody to know what it meant to him.

Kissing the top of his head, she said, 'Did you forget to pack something? Is that why you came back home for a minute?' Jonah's words had been prophetic.

'No. I had a stomach-ache, but it's gone now.'

'Good. Because I thought I'd microwave some popcorn for everyone and take it to Jeff's with us.'

'Yippee! I'll get it out!'

Sarah followed after him, grabbing a pillow from her bed and a quilt that had seen better days from the linen-closet. Even though it was September, the heat still stayed in the lower nineties during the day, which meant the nights were balmy. She wouldn't need anything else.

By the time Jonah walked into the kitchen from the back door, announcing he was ready to drive them to Jeff's, they'd managed to pop four bags of popcorn. Avoiding Jonah's eyes, Sarah turned off lights and locked up while they carried everything to the car.

Jonah had pulled his Jaguar to the side of the access road—a material reminder of his legendary business acumen which separated him from other men. After opening the passenger door for her, he helped Brody into the back seat, then walked around the front of his car and got in.

Brody put his head between them from behind, as if they were a family out for a drive. Sarah's heart kept up its furious pounding. She was afraid that in the luxurious leather confines of Jonah's car, he could hear it.

'Which way to Jeff's, Brody?'

'Keep going till I tell you to stop.'

'That's easy enough.' He started the engine and engaged the gears. 'Who else is sleeping over?'

'Bruce and Kevin and T.J. Kevin's mad because he's not in your class.' Brody leaned forward and tapped Jonah's shoulder. 'You have to turn here, then you can park in front.'

As soon as they rounded the corner Sarah could see a couple of tents on the lawn in front of the Masons' townhouse. When Jonah pulled up to the curb, the boys scrambled out of the larger one and ran up to the car. The second they saw their teacher, they all shouted his name and jumped up and down. Jonah worked his magic with everyone.

'Can I take the popcorn to the tent, Mom?'

'Sure. That's what it's for.'

'Not so fast,' Jonah inserted, plucking one sack from Brody's arms. 'This is for your mother and me.'

Silence followed in the children's wake, and suddenly Sarah felt self-conscious, but she needed to talk to Jonah before he got out of the car and was besieged by the boys who obviously adored him.

'Jonah?'

At the sound of her voice, he jerked his head around. In the near-darkness, which was relieved only by a streetlamp on the adjacent parking bay, she thought maybe she'd misread the cold stare he turned on her. But his next words confirmed her suspicion.

'Save it, Mrs Brown. Tonight you've made your son ecstatic. Tomorrow you can tear into me, but, if I were you, I'd check my facts before sending me more hate-mail. Lynette picked Brody's name out of a hat to ride in that fire truck. However, I refuse to apologize for being happy about it.'

CHAPTER FIVE

ON THAT terse note he levered himself from the car and went around back to get their things.

Sarah deserved his contempt. But she also knew she had to do something to cool his anger or she wouldn't be able to act or behave normally the rest of the night.

Climbing out of the passenger side, she caught up with him just as he closed the trunk, his arms loaded. 'Jonah—— Please——' she said urgently.

His gaze narrowed on her mouth. 'Please, what?'

The way he was looking at her made her tremble. 'I—I want to thank you for being honest with me about Brody. I had no idea what I've been doing to him. If I get the chance tonight, I'll tell him why I've cried so much, and assure him that my life would be over without him.'

His facial features tautened. 'The best present you could give him would be to stop.' She averted her eyes guiltily and heard his sharp intake of breath. 'Apparently that's asking the impossible.'

Not giving her a chance to explain, he strode toward the boys, who converged on him with shrieks of delight, Brody's being the loudest.

They couldn't have cared less about Sarah, who was too shaken by the emotion in Jonah's voice to enter the mêlée. Obviously he believed she couldn't overcome her grief and was disgusted by it because of the damage it was doing to Brody.

Sarah had to admit that there'd been a time, even as recently as half a year ago, when she'd wondered if she was doomed to live out the rest of her life in a permanent state of mourning. But the plans for the move to Colorado, the changes in Brody, had brought her out of the worst of her depression.

If anything, the tears of late had had more to do with guilt, the guilt she suffered for having fought with Rich so much in the last year before his death over his determination to stay in the coast guard. His fatal accident had been so pointless, so needless. It had robbed Brody of a father who had never seen very much of him as it was.

This summer there'd been actual moments when she blamed herself for marrying Rich because in the end it hadn't been fair to Brody, who deserved a father who would be around to watch him grow into a man, to teach him how to be one.

And, of late, she'd shed angry tears because Rich's parents still hadn't phoned or sent one letter. She'd seen the way Brody had behaved for the first year after the memorial service. He would watch for the mailman and race to get the phone before she did, hoping that maybe this time his grandparents would remember him. But, after this long without any word, Brody had finally given up hope.

She'd even cried tears of frustration because of her vague resentment against her brother-in-law.

Hal was a nice enough man, but he was too self-centered and meticulous about his person to put up with animals or children, let alone Brody whom he considered a handful.

If Hal had taken any interest in Brody, any at all, it might have hastened the healing process for her son, but that wasn't meant to be.

It appeared that the only man in Brody's life who could make a difference right now was Jonah Sinclair, and, so far, Sarah had done everything in her power to prevent a relationship from developing because—— Sarah couldn't honestly give a reason. She only knew that Jonah was no ordinary man, that her son had done a complete turnabout since school had started.

While they erected his dome tent she watched all of them interact, and could sense a bond between Brody and Jonah.

Though he had fun and teased the other boys, she saw the way he'd suddenly ruffle Brody's hair, or flash him an encouraging smile in an off moment. Most of all, she noticed a tenderness in his eyes when they rested on her son, a tenderness that brought a lump to her throat because Brody needed affection from a man like Jonah so badly.

She couldn't bear to think what would happen when he went away. Only three and a half months left till Christmas. Brody's heart would be broken beyond repair.

The only way she could think to offset his hold over her son was to start dating again. Her work as a legal researcher brought her in contact with a dozen law firms at least. She'd had many opportunities to meet men since the move, but always found a reason to put them off because she wasn't ready yet, and because she feared Brody's reaction.

To her surprise, there were a number of eligible bachelors moving up the corporate ladder who'd asked her out, knowing full well she was a widow with a seven-year-old son. Several of them were quite attractive and had suggested activities which could include Brody.

She'd be seeing John Marsden on Tuesday and Rand Hanks on Wednesday, and knew they'd press her again for a commitment. Maybe this time she'd take them up on it, and make certain Brody was included so he'd feel an integral part of her life. It would be good for him to see another masculine face besides Jonah's.

Filled with fresh resolve and direction she joined Patsy, who welcomed her with open arms. Together they distributed the rest of popcorn and cans of soda while Jonah chatted privately with Jeff's father, Greg. Sarah couldn't help but wonder what the two of them were talking about.

After a few more games of tag and frisbee, Greg told the boys they were starting to disturb the neighbors so it was time to bed down for the night.

For once, his suggestion met with everyone's approval, since the whole point of the exercise was to sleep outside in a tent.

Brody came running over to Sarah. Jonah followed closely behind. 'Jonah says you're going to sleep in his tent tonight.'

'That's right.' She smiled without looking at Jonah, pretending that she knew everything going on in his mind, when in reality she was swimming way over her head. 'But if I get scared, can I come in with you guys?'

His face screwed up and he looked at Jonah. 'No girls are allowed, are they.' It was a rhetorical question.

'No,' he murmured in his deep voice. 'But I bet your mom won't mind if you crawl in with her—if she screams, that is.'

'Yeah. She's scared of mice and spiders.'

'*Brody*! You're not supposed to tell people my secrets. It's embarrassing.'

'Jonah's not people.'

No. He's someone who has already become far too important to you.

'Are you going to be all right, Sarah?'

She nodded to Jonah, aware of emotions churning inside of her she could do nothing about.

'I put your things inside the tent. I also left a sleeping-bag and a flashlight.'

Finally she found the courage to meet his penetrating glance. 'Thank you——' her voice shook '—for everything.' She meant it. While she'd been in a world of her own, trying to survive, Jonah had had the advantage of seeing the whole picture, and had been able to let her know what was going on inside Brody.

'Don't speak too soon,' he murmured cryptically. 'You still have a whole night to get through.'

'Yeah.' Brody grinned, tuning in to the hidden nuance of meaning. 'Goodnight, Mom.' He reached up and pecked her cheek.

'Goodnight, honey. Be good and don't stay up too late. Tell the boys they can come to our house for bacon and scones in the morning.'

'Yippee! Hey—guys!'

As he ran off, Jonah murmured, 'Keep this up and I might join them.'

She rubbed her arms vigorously. 'If giving you a meal could pay the debt I owe you, I'd fix them for you indefinitely.'

His face became an inscrutable mask. 'Don't make rash promises you can't keep. But I'll hold you to one breakfast of bacon and scones, since I can't remember the last time anyone made them for me.'

Long after he'd gone back to check on the boys and she'd settled down in his sleeping-bag, Jonah's comment kept going around in her head. Had he been referring to the fact that he'd been divorced for a long time?

She found herself wondering about his ex-wife. Somewhere Sarah had read that a divorce caused pretty much the same stress and pain as the death of a spouse. If that was true, then Jonah had been through agony just as she had.

He'd mentioned that his former wife lived in Hawaii, but he'd said nothing about children. If he did have a son or daughter, she couldn't imagine how he stood to be apart from them.

Maybe his experience as a parent had helped him to become such an expert psychologist. But, if he was a parent, then living thousands of miles away would make visitation difficult. She surmised that that was what he'd been doing before he'd flown in from San Diego that first night.

With so many unanswered questions, Sarah wasn't the least bit tired. On impulse she moved her pillow outside the opening of the tent, the better to see and hear the boys, who seemed to have fallen asleep. Secure because she was there, Brody had been able to settle down at last.

Without Jonah's intervention she had no idea how long she might have gone on before she'd picked up on her son's fears. She would always be grateful to Jonah for that.

But it still didn't change the fact that the more time Brody spent in his teacher's company, the more painful it would be for her son when it came time to say goodbye.

A shudder racked her body and she turned on her back to gaze up at the stars. It had been a long time, too long in fact, since she'd taken the time to enjoy nature. For some reason tonight, she felt very much alive.

While she fingered the grass she listened to the crickets and breathed in the night air, which still carried the wonderful smell of summer. Was it mock orange or honeysuckle she could detect? Whatever the scent, it made her yearn for something she couldn't put a name to. She felt an ache clear to the palms of her hands.

When she finally felt herself getting sleepy, she inched her way back inside, pulled the quilt over her shoulders and closed her eyes.

At some point she drifted off and didn't know anything else until she heard a sound against the tent-flap.

'Brody?' she murmured groggily. 'Is that you, honey? Come here. You can sleep with me.' She instinctively lifted an arm to pull him down to her and encountered a luxuriant head of hair. The texture felt so different from Brody's that she loved running her fingers through it. Until she came in contact with a firm male jaw. The slight rasp against her palm made her gasp and she sat up, pushing the hair out of her eyes.

'Jonah?' she whispered in shock, shaken by his nearness and her response to the feel of his hair and skin beneath her fingertips.

His outline was a mere silhouette in the darkness. 'I came over to say goodnight.'

'You're leaving?' It was out before she realized how disappointed she must have sounded to him. 'But the boys——'

'They're dead to the world, and I still have work to do before my staff goes back to California tomorrow. Greg will run you home in the morning.

Don't worry about my tent and bag. I'll get my things later.'

She couldn't believe how much it mattered to her that he wouldn't be spending the rest of the night with them. She was as bad as Brody. What in heaven's name was wrong with her?

'D-Does that mean you won't be wanting breakfast after all?' The question slipped out before she could catch herself.

'Why?' he drawled with heavy sarcasm. 'Are you regretting your impulsive offer already?'

'No, of course not.'

After another uneasy silence he said, 'I didn't mention anything to you earlier about zipping your tent closed because I've been keeping an eye on you. But now that I'm leaving, make sure you're shut in tight. There's a little window you can open for air.'

Her eyes rounded. He'd been watching her the whole time?

'You thought I was Brody just now, but it could have been anyone.' His voice hardened, driving the point home. 'Before they could get to you, they'd have to open two sets of zippers, which would give you enough time to decide if you want company.'

At his mocking tone, her whole body suffused with heat, reminding her of that moment when she'd reached out for her son and found Jonah instead. No longer able to lie to herself, she realized that the reason she hadn't pulled away from him instantly was because she'd wanted to prolong the contact. She'd wanted to touch him.

As a sort of emotional safety blanket, she hugged the pillow to her chest and whispered, 'Thank you for the warning.'

'I don't want you to be frightened, just cautious. Brody tells me you've never camped out before.'

She prayed he couldn't hear the pounding of her heart. 'No, I haven't.'

'Under the right conditions, there's nothing like it.'

'I wouldn't have missed this. Tonight the sky is spectacular.'

'I noticed,' he said in a barely audible whisper. 'But if you want to see something truly miraculous, you need to camp at twelve thousand feet, away from the city lights.'

She stirred restlessly. 'I—I've heard the mountains are the best place to study the heavens. Rich kept promisi——'

But Sarah never finished what she was going to say because Jonah unexpectedly got to his feet outside the tent, the brief rapport she'd felt with him gone.

She'd spoken without thinking, and shouldn't have brought Rich's name into the conversation. It had just slipped out, but she was certain Jonah had construed it as a sick preoccupation with the past, because she heard the sardonic edge to his deep voice when he said, 'Leave the tent-flap open at your own risk.' Seconds later she heard the low purring sound of a motor.

On an audible groan, Sarah buried her face in the pillow, wishing she could call him back and explain. She had only herself to blame for shattering the fragile camaraderie between them.

To be able to carry on an exchange not punctuated by mutual antagonism had been like a dream. Unfortunately the dream was elusive, and, now that she was awake, the let-down was much greater than she would have believed.

Somehow, all the excitement and adventure seemed to have gone out of the night. As she got up to fasten the flap and open a window she had the awful premonition that Jonah had everything to do with the yawning emptiness she was experiencing now.

The rest of the night became an agony she had to endure. Around dawn she finally dropped off, but that was the moment the boys in the other tent made enough noise to waken the dead.

'Where's Jonah?' she heard Brody cry. Naturally he was the first one to notice, she moaned to herself.

It didn't take long for her son to invade her tent, wanting to know what had happened to his idol. She sat up and rubbed her eyes. 'He had some work to do, but he should be over later for breakfast.' Unless he's too disgusted with me to bother, she added inwardly. 'Did you have fun?' She held out her arms.

Brody lunged for her, almost knocking her over. 'This was the best, Mom! Now can we go home and make scones? Jonah said he could eat a hundred of 'em.'

At the mention of Jonah's name, her eyes closed tightly. 'I think we'll have to wait for Jeff's dad, honey. It's still early and he's probably sleeping.'

'No, he's not. Jeff went to wake him up.'

Muttering something about there being no rest for the wicked, Sarah staggered to her feet and slipped on her sandals.

Within an hour and a half, Sarah had gone to the grocery store and was back at the condo, making preparations to feed the horde.

Once the food frenzy started, it was nonstop, and Sarah was thrilled to note that Brody eagerly devoured a half-dozen scones along with the rest of them, his concern over Jonah's absence apparently forgotten.

But in that assumption she was wrong, because when the phone rang, Brody practically knocked over his chair to answer it before she could.

'Jonah?' she heard him say after he'd lifted the receiver. He knew better than to answer the phone that way, but anticipation had made him forget and the excitement in his voice tore at her heartstrings.

Fortunately there was too much noise in the background for anyone else to notice, but Sarah watched the way his face fell as he handed her the phone. 'It's for you.'

To her surprise, John Marsden was on the line, telling her he couldn't wait until Tuesday because there was a new development in the case and he needed her help right away, if she could get started on it Monday morning.

After watching Brody's dejection, which to her chagrin had echoed her own, she decided now would be as good a time as any to put her plan into action, particularly since it was evident Jonah wouldn't be coming for breakfast after all.

Turning her back to Brody, who at this point was keeping a constant eye out the window for signs of Jonah, she invited John to drop by. They'd discuss things further over scones. On impulse, she told him to bring his bathing-suit. Today was the last day the pool would be open. After they'd finished their work, the three of them could go swimming.

John's reaction left her in no doubt that this was what he'd been wanting for a long time. He told her he'd be over in an hour, saying something about a barbecue he'd like to take her to the following Friday evening. Other children would be there and she could bring Brody if she wanted.

As soon as she hung up the phone guilt assailed her, because she'd led John to believe she was interested when it wasn't the truth. But the situation required desperate measures. Somehow she had to counteract Jonah's influence on Brody. Short of moving back to San Diego, she didn't know another way to do it.

The phone call seemed to mark the end of the festivities. Jeff's parents thanked Sarah for the fabulous meal, then announced they were taking all the boys back to their place to start the clean-up and put away the tents.

Sarah sensed Brody's reluctance to go anywhere without Jonah, but she stood firm, reminding him he had a responsibility to do his share of the work, otherwise there would be no more sleepovers.

On a happier note she told him they'd go swimming later in the day. That seemed to cheer him up a little, probably because he hoped to see Jonah at the pool.

Sarah could have told Brody that Jonah had an important business conference and wouldn't be available, but now was not the time. Nor did she feel it the right moment to say anything about John. Instinct warned her to proceed carefully in that department, and play it by ear as the day unfolded.

Within the hour Sarah had cleaned up the kitchen, taken a shower, and had put on a modest pair of walking shorts and a blouse. When John arrived he was all smiles, bringing a new energy with him that made her feel guiltier than ever.

She'd put the scones on the coffee table in the living-room so he could help himself while they worked, informing him that, when Brody came home from Jeff's, they'd take a break and go over to the pool.

At that point John mentioned something about taking in dinner and a movie later that night, but

Sarah quickly declined, sorry that she'd ever started this.

A look of disappointment crossed over his face, but he took the news well enough, then proceeded to extract a tentative commitment from her for the following Friday night. His tenacity probably made him a good courtroom lawyer, she thought.

Finally they were able to get down to business and worked companionably for the next half-hour. When the buzzer sounded, Sarah realized that Greg must have dropped Brody off in front, and she hurried to the door to let him in.

'Hi, honey. You're just in time to meet——' But nothing else came out, because a pair of direct, uncompromising brown eyes collided with hers, sending her pulse racing at harrowing speed. Jonah.

He murmured a greeting, but his laser-like gaze zeroed in on John, who by this time was lounging on the floor in front of the coffee table, finishing a scone. Jonah's eyes flicked back to hers, an unsettling glitter pinning her to the spot. 'It appears I'm too late after all.'

She shook her head and on a shaky breath said, 'No, you're not. There are plenty of scones left. Come in.'

After a perceptible pause, Jonah entered the house, looking larger than life and frankly forbidding. He shut the door, his eyes never leaving hers.

Sarah stood there in a stupor, consumed by warring emotions of fear and excitement. 'John

Marsden, meet Jonah Sinclair,' she explained nervously. 'John just dropped by to discuss a case. He's working out a strategy for me.'

'Umm—so it seems,' Jonah drawled insinuatingly. Suddenly he lifted a hand to her face and caught at a dab of jam on her softly rounded chin. His touch sent a major shockwave through her body. 'I couldn't resist,' he said in a husky tone before tasting his finger.

Sarah's knees nearly buckled in reaction. By this time, John, who couldn't possibly have missed the by-play, had gotten up from the floor, visibly bristling, not only from Jonah's aggression, but the liberty he'd taken with Sarah.

'Did any other nocturnal visitors bother you after I left your tent last night?' Jonah whispered the intimate question loud enough for John to hear.

Sarah wished the floor would simply swallow her up, and turned jerkily to John to make an explanation. 'J-Jonah is Brody's school teacher. Last night he joined some of the boys and neighbors for a sleepover, but he had to leave early. I fixed breakfast for everyone this morning and told him to come by any time for his.'

'You teach school?' John's condescending courtroom persona came to the fore, but he was no match for Jonah. Sarah had it in her heart to feel sorry for the attorney, who could have no idea of the kind of man he was up against.

'I do,' Jonah answered in his deep, confident voice. 'I've discovered that the classroom is a far more challenging arena than the courtroom. There's nothing like the honesty of a child to keep one's wits rapier-sharp.'

A covert glance at John's mutinous expression and Sarah panicked. 'Look, John—I'll just feed Jonah and then we'll go swimming.'

'Don't mind me,' Jonah inserted mildly. 'It isn't as if I haven't been in your kitchen before. While I fry up some bacon, you two go ahead and do whatever you were doing when I interrupted you.'

He disappeared from the room, leaving a shell-shocked Sarah to deal with John, who looked as if he couldn't take much more. 'Why don't we leave everything as is, and go over to the pool now?'

John trained a faintly accusing gaze on Sarah. 'Are you sure that's what you want?'

'Of course.'

After hesitating, he muttered his assent and said, 'We'll go over in my car.'

'Good,' she said in relief. 'Wait a moment while I get my suit and towel.'

In a few minutes she started for the living-room with her things, praying nothing else could go wrong. To her surprise she could hear Brody's animated voice. He'd come home without her knowing it.

'Mom——' he cried when he saw her and rushed over to give her a hug. 'Jonah's back and he wants us to go swimming with him. Is that okay?'

The smile which had been missing at breakfast had slipped back in place. On the periphery of her vision she could see John near the front door. While she'd been getting ready Jonah had wandered into the living-room, and stood in place devouring several scones with obvious relish. The tension was so thick Sarah felt she might lose control at any second.

'Brody—I—I want you to meet John Marsden, an attorney here in town.'

'Jonah already introduced us.'

Biting her lip, she said, 'I invited him to go swimming with us.'

Brody shrugged. 'That's okay. You don't care if he comes, do you, Jonah?'

Jonah drained a full glass of orange juice, then muttered, 'Not at all.'

Furious at him for taking such brazen advantage of the situation, she said to Brody, 'John has invited you and me to a barbecue next Friday night at one of his friends' homes.'

'That's awfully nice of you, John,' Jonah inserted in a deceptively civil tone, 'but I'm afraid Sarah will have to take a raincheck. I've arranged for my class to watch the San Diego Chargers slaughter the Broncos next Friday night. We have third and fourth row seats on the fifty-yard line and Sarah is one of the room mothers committed to helping me.'

CHAPTER SIX

'YIPPEE!' Brody shouted. 'Mom—did you hear that? I'm going to my first Broncos game!'

'That's very exciting, Brody, but right now we're going swimming.' Sarah struggled to keep her voice steady. This was the first she'd heard of Jonah's proposed outing, one guaranteed to win every student's undying affection, but none more than Brody's whose adoration of Jonah had already grown out of hand. 'Get your suit. We're driving over to the pool in John's car.'

Her son started to protest but she forestalled him. 'You can swim with Jonah another day.'

'But the pool's closing today.' Brody looked as if he was on the verge of tears.

Sarah's eyes swerved to the man who'd managed to turn her world inside-out, warning him to go along with this or else.

Vastly relieved when she saw Jonah move toward the front door and open it, she wasn't prepared for his next words, which shook her to the foundations.

'I'll tell you what, Brody,' he said in that deep, inimicable voice of his, 'since we already went swimming the other day, what do you say if we go over to the game-room some time next week and play a little ping-pong. Talk it over with your mother, and let me know what you decide.'

His dark, inscrutable gaze impaled Sarah with a mesmerising power she couldn't escape. 'Sorry I was late for breakfast. It was delicious.'

Almost as an afterthought, he darted a cursory glance to the other man and said, 'Nice meeting you, Marsden.' As soon as he disappeared out the door, Brody broke into uninhibited shrieks of joy.

In her whole life, Sarah had never come so close to fainting. 'Brody——' she called a halt to his embarrassing display of excitement in front of John. 'Go get your suit, please. We'll talk about this later.'

'Okay, Mom.' He skipped off, his face radiant with anticipation of the week to come.

'Sarah?'

At the sound of John's sober voice, her head jerked around guiltily. 'I—I'm sorry about all this,' she murmured, spreading her hands in dismay. 'I had no idea Brody's teacher would show up this late.'

She watched him rub the back of his head in what looked like frustration. 'Why did you bother to let me think you were interested in me? The man made it blatantly clear I'm trespassing on his private property.'

Her face colored. 'I—I know how it looked, but it isn't what you think.'

'I have eyes, Sarah. And feelings,' he added in a quieter tone. 'I'm not talking about your son, who obviously worships the ground he walks on.

I'm talking about you and the way you reacted when he showed up on your doorstep. Hell, in the last couple of months, if you'd ever once reacted that same way around me, I'd have done something about my feelings for you long before now.'

'John—you don't understand,' she cried out, appalled because her emotions were so transparent, and feeling guilt-ridden for giving John hope when she knew the chemistry wasn't there.

'I understand more than you give me credit for,' he murmured resignedly. 'Let's be honest here. I've been waiting to make a move on you because I knew you were still trying to get over your husband's death. When you invited me to come swimming today, I broke a date with someone else to be with you.'

Mortified, Sarah averted her eyes. 'I'm so sorry.'

'So am I, because I'm too late. Another man has already managed to accomplish what I couldn't do.'

She shook her head. 'You're wrong, John.'

'You weren't standing in my shoes, Sarah. When he came through that door, the two of you created enough chemistry to blot out everything and everyone else in the room. I could have cut it with a knife. To say that I was *de trop* doesn't begin to describe it.'

'No, John. Please don't go,' she urged, plagued by remorse as she watched him gather up his things and put them in his briefcase.

His hands stilled and he looked at her. 'I'd stay if I thought you meant it, but you don't. You're only trying to be polite, so let's get back to a professional footing. You're a good researcher and I don't want to lose you. Can I expect you on Monday?'

She swallowed hard. 'Of course.'

'Good. I'll let myself out.'

After he'd gone, Sarah stood there in a state of complete turmoil. Her plan to introduce a new man into their lives had backfired with disastrous results.

It was Jonah's fault.

Like taking candy from a baby, he'd known exactly what he was doing when he breezed into the condo and manipulated Brody to accomplish his objective without regard to anyone else's feelings—least of all John's. No doubt Jonah had applied the same ruthless tactics to put his company on top and keep it there.

But this wasn't business.

This was *her* life. Brody was *her* son. Jonah had no right to toy with them.

Her hands balled into fists. Because of Jonah's interference, John's friendship and backing had been placed at risk. After what had just happened, she realized what a decent person John was to still want her to work for him. Never again would she allow Jonah an opportunity to disrupt their lives any more than he already had.

Her chest heaving, she cried, 'Brody?'

'I'm ready,' he answered in a sullen tone, and wandered, head down, into the living-room in his T-shirt, wearing his swimsuit under his shorts. His pathetic demeanor was the result of Jonah's handiwork.

Her anger kindled, she said, 'We're not going swimming quite yet.'

'We're not?' He lifted his head and looked around. 'Where's that man?'

'Something came up and Mr Marsden had to go home.'

'Yippee!' Brody jumped up and down, his face wreathed in a brilliant smile. 'Now we can swim with Jonah!'

She'd been bracing herself for that response. 'No, Brody,' she cautioned. 'Right now I want you to settle down in front of the TV and watch a couple of cartoons while I go talk to Jonah.'

His eyes grew huge. 'You're going to Jonah's? Why can't I come?'

'Because this is a matter for grownups.'

She could hear his mind working it out. 'How long are you going to stay over there?'

'Not long. Five minutes at the most.'

'Okay,' he muttered, scuffing the tip of his shoe back and forth on the rug. 'But I still don't see wh——'

'Brody——' she warned. 'Lock the kitchen door behind me and don't let anyone in. I'll hurry.' She kissed his forehead before leaving the condo through the back door.

With a sense of *déjà vu*, she headed for Jonah's townhouse, hoping to catch him before he went somewhere else. Adrenaline lent her wings as she darted through the carport to the access road.

As she rounded the curve one of the heel-less sandals she'd put on with her shorts and T-shirt came off. She had to go back for it, and took off the other sandal before running barefoot the rest of the way.

Relieved to see that his Jaguar was still in its parking spot, she rushed toward the back door and almost collided with Jonah, who unexpectedly stepped outside carrying what looked like a rolled-up foam rubber pad under one arm.

'Oh——' she gasped softly as her hand brushed against the solid strength of his forearm. Even that brief contact sent an electrifying surge of warmth through her body. She quickly backed away from him, too out of breath to say anything for a minute.

Jonah's dark eyes swept over her in intimate appraisal, taking in her bare feet and the rapid rise and fall of her chest until color stormed her cheeks. Then his brows furrowed in silent mockery.

'I presume your washer is flooding the kitchen again. Surely the esteemed counselor who's been lounging on the living-room floor with you for the last couple of hours is capable of turning off the water?'

Her proud chin lifted a fraction. 'I won't dignify that remark with a comment. You know exactly why I'm here.'

'I do,' he murmured in a deep voice, 'and when you're ready to let go of your anger, *you'll* know the reason why, too.'

After that cryptic aside, she had to clamp down hard on her temper. 'What you did today cost me a friend and could have ruined my business relationship with John's firm.'

His mouth quirked unpleasantly. 'Which means the poor devil has already gone home to lick his wounds. I wouldn't have credited him with that much sense.' He stepped past her to fit the pad in the trunk of his car.

Sarah was appalled. 'Why did you do it, Jonah?'

He shut the lid before studying her taut features for an overly long moment. 'More to the point, why don't you ask yourself why you bothered to encourage him, when we both know he never had a hope in hell with you in the first place.'

The truth of his words put her in a white-hot rage, causing her to twist the inset strap on one of her sandals until it snapped.

The sound brought a glimmer of satisfaction to Jonah's eyes, inflaming her further.

'Doesn't being the head of a world-renowned, multi-million-dollar corporation give you enough challenge and stimulation without having to resort to such cruel machinations?' Her voice grew more shrill. 'What you did was unconscionable, because you used Brody's affection to make certain John felt inadequate.'

He moved around to the driver's side of the car and rested his back against the door, his stance intimidating because it brought him much closer to her. She wanted to run as far away as possible from him, but remained in the same spot because she would have hated giving him that bit of satisfaction.

'Correct me if I'm wrong, but, as I recall, you invited me to breakfast. In fact, you said something about providing it indefinitely.'

'That was before you took over my home and insulted my guest.' Her voice shook.

'Somebody had to put the blind fool out of his misery. When you analyze it, my method was kinder because it ended his pain sooner.'

'So you took it upon yourself to do the honors,' she scathed, riddled with self-recrimination because she should never have involved John in anything to do with Jonah.

A dangerous glitter lit Jonah's eyes, giving him a slightly menacing air. 'Don't you know that there's nothing more crippling to the male psyche than to be flattered by a woman's interest only to wake up one day and discover you meant less than nothing to her, that you'd been used for whatever purpose she deemed suitable at the time?'

'You sound as if you're speaking from experience,' she taunted with relish. 'What's the matter? Did your wife wake up one day and decide all your millions weren't enough anymore?' She flung the question at him, then shivered uncontrollably, because a frightening stillness had come over Jonah, making him appear unnervingly ruthless.

Too late she realized that regardless of the provocation there was no excuse on her part for such vicious insensitivity. She could have cut her tongue out.

'Your construction of my disastrous marriage is on the right track but doesn't go far enough.' His voice seemed to come out of some dark, hidden cavern.

He reminded her of a magnificent jungle cat, who'd stalked his prey into an inescapable position and was getting ready to tear it apart.

'My wife *did* wake up one day, unhappily pregnant with another man's child.'

At that painful revelation Sarah clutched her stomach, and wished to heaven she'd never started this.

'I knew it couldn't possibly be mine,' he said with bitter irony. 'A football injury to my spleen years earlier made it impossible for me to give her one.'

Dear God.

'Unfortunately, she had no idea who the father was. As it turned out, she'd had multiple partners, but assured me none of them meant anything to her.'

Sarah couldn't bear to hear anymore. '*Jonah*——'

'I could have forgiven her for all of it, and raised the child as my own.' He kept on talking, as if he hadn't heard her cry out his name. 'After all, in marrying me, she was deprived of ever having a baby from her own body. Since it was my fault——'

'That isn't anyone's fault!' Sarah defended, with a ferocity that surprised even her, but she was feeling utterly helpless, because she wanted to find that wounded place inside of him and comfort him.

Jonah's eyes had been trained on her, but he was seeing something else, someone else in his mind, filling Sarah with an emptiness too wretched to describe. Something told her he'd never accept comfort from a woman again, particularly not Sarah. Too much damage had been done.

'I decided to overlook her infidelity, which seems to be a by-product of most marriages these days. And I *had* vowed to love her for better or for worse...' His voice trailed with a self-denigration that tore at her heartstrings.

'But, the moment my back was turned, she took the opportunity to end her pregnancy.'

'No——' Sarah whispered in horror.

The bleakness in his dark eyes devastated her. 'Her thinking was so twisted that she believed in aborting her child and promising to remain faithful for the rest of our mortal existence, she could stay married to me.'

'Don't——' she pleaded with him, but he was too far gone to listen.

'She even threw in the forgotten promise that we could adopt children, something we'd agreed upon before we got married. Fool that I was, I believed her in those early days of innocence. Before the veil was ripped from my eyes,' he added on a caustic note.

She gasped softly when she realized he was staring at her with an accusatory gleam. 'Like a revelation, it came to me that her early avowals of love, her willingness to adopt children out of that love, were only a smoke-screen to reach her real objective.

'The bald truth is, no other man of her acquaintance ever could or will be able to keep her in the same lifestyle I've provided over the last five years with "all my millions".'

His painful reminder of the cruel question Sarah had hurtled at him earlier filled her with unspeakable sorrow.

'Forgive me for saying that,' she begged, moving closer. 'I didn't mean it,' she averred, reaching out unthinkingly to touch his arm. 'You know I didn't.'

'Do I?' he muttered with an understated savagery, eyeing her hand, which she quickly removed. But not before he flashed her a mirthless smile that didn't reach his eyes.

'Jonah—I was angry with you be—because, in the few weeks that I've known you, you've made me come face to face with myself.' She had difficulty swallowing. 'It hasn't been a pretty sight.'

Far too aware of his physical proximity and her vulnerability to that potent masculine appeal, she backed away from him, clutching her sandals in a death-grip.

Afraid to face his stony gaze, she averted her eyes. 'You were right about John. I shouldn't have tried to force something that wasn't there from the beginning.'

An uneasy silence fell between them. 'Well, that's something, at least.' His voice grated. 'Now you'll have to excuse me.'

Dismissing her without a qualm, because he didn't need or want anything more from her, he disappeared inside the open door of the condo.

His rebuff was more painful than she would have believed. Compelled to repair some of the damage and smooth the friction between them, she followed him to the door where she could see him pouring ice into a small cooler.

'Wh-Where are you going?'

'Away—for what's left of the weekend.'

She suspected he'd head for the mountains and camp out in some isolated spot. Not wanting him to leave like this, with nothing resolved between them, she ventured, 'Brody knew I was coming over here. He was hoping to swim with you this afternoon.'

To her shock he wheeled around, his eyes blazing with an angry light. 'What in the hell are you playing at now? Serving your child up to me out of some misguided sense of pity?' He let out a stream of profanity that left her so shaken she had to hold on to the doorjamb for support.

'You're wasting your time,' he sneered. 'Go home to your son, Sarah. Curl up with your photo albums and your memories. Leave me to mine.'

In an economy of movement he left the kitchen for another part of the condo. It was her cue to exit, but she couldn't bring herself to do it. She didn't want to.

Employing Jonah's tactics, she reached for the wall phone and punched in her own number, praying that what she was about to do wouldn't turn into another catastrophe.

'Brody?' she whispered when he answered.

'Mom?'

'Yes. Turn off the TV and run over to Jonah's as fast as you can. Make sure you lock the door behind you.'

'Yippee!'

His euphoria was so great, he slammed the receiver down with a crash, and it almost broke her eardrum.

Drawing a deep breath, because of the huge risk she was taking, she slipped outside and got into the front passenger seat of the Jaguar.

So far Jonah hadn't made an appearance. She prayed Brody would make it over before Jonah discovered she hadn't gone away and ordered her out of his car.

She was counting on his affection for Brody to defuse an already volatile situation, and could have cried for joy when she saw her dark-headed son scrambling along the access road as fast as his short legs would carry him.

As he ran up to the car she leaned across the gearshift and called to him through the driver's open window. 'Brody, honey?'

He was puffing. 'Where's Jonah?'

'Inside the house. Go find him and tell him we're ready.'

'Are we going over to the pool?'

'No.' Her mouth curved in a secret smile. 'He had so much fun last night he didn't want it to end, so he's taking us camping in the mountains.'

Brody's eyes pulsated like hot blue stars. Too overjoyed to speak, he raced into the condo shouting Jonah's name at the top of his lungs. No doubt everyone in Birchwood South could hear him, but for once Sarah didn't care.

Her heart pounded unmercifully when moments later she saw Jonah's tall figure emerge from the house with Brody trailing him, his small hands pulling a dark green duffle bag that was bigger than he was.

He was chattering away blithely, his adoring eyes trained on the man who ignored Sarah as if she weren't there and gave her son instructions as they worked together to load the trunk with the rest of the camping gear.

Sarah could have gone inside to bring out the cooler, but, remembering that possession was nine-tenths of the law, she opted to stay put. That way

Jonah would have to extricate her physically from the car if he wanted her to leave.

At Jonah's bidding, Brody scurried back into the condo for some pillows. Thinking that he'd engineered it so her son would leave them alone, Sarah braced herself for an ugly confrontation.

But, as she was coming to find out, Jonah was not a predictable man. Instead of ripping into her, he worked at a steady pace with Brody, moving back and forth while he patiently answered her son's thousand and one questions in that low, unforgettable voice.

Finally they were ready, and Brody scurried into the back seat of the plush car. Unable to refrain from looking at him, Sarah peered through her dark lashes as Jonah locked up the condo and headed for them.

Their eyes met briefly through the front windshield. His were indecipherable.

Once he'd levered himself behind the wheel and closed the door, he turned his head, taking in the skimpy shorts and T-shirt she was wearing until she felt exposed and hot all over.

'I don't have time to wait for the two of you to pack,' he murmured in level tones, staring pointedly at the broken sandal on her left foot. 'It gets cold after the sun goes down. Are you sure this is what you want to do? I'm not coming back until tomorrow afternoon.'

Because she'd never been camping, he thought he could scare her off, but she wasn't about to back down now. Not until she'd had a chance really to talk to Jonah, and clear the air between them. But that couldn't happen until much later, when Brody had gone to bed for the night.'

'We don't have anything else to do, do we, Mom?' Brody's voice held a hint of anxiety.

'No,' she answered firmly.

'Yippee!'

With that one word, she'd committed them. If Jonah was shocked, he didn't let it show.

'So be it,' he mocked drily, as if to say that since she was foolish enough to come along totally unprepared, then he wasn't going to be responsible for the consequences.

Sarah wasn't too concerned. Though he might make her suffer for the brazen way she'd insinuated herself into taking this trip with him, invading his privacy, she knew deep in her heart that he'd never punish Brody for her failings.

'Fasten your seatbelts.'

Sarah heard a click.

'Okay,' Brody called out. 'Mine's done.'

She followed suit, flashing Jonah a guileless smile his eyes acknowledged with a mysterious glint that made her breathless and sent a thrill of alarm through her body.

But it was too late to back out now. With practised ease, he swung the car into reverse, then switched gears, guiding the car along the access road to the exit of the complex.

Seconds later they merged with the street traffic and headed for the freeway. While Brody continued to ply Jonah with questions about their destination, Sarah noted that he drove with the same confidence and authority he did everything else.

She enjoyed watching the play of his broad shoulders, the tan of his strong arms with their dusting of dark golden hairs. Her gaze darted to his capable hands, whose long fingers were ringless. She wondered if he'd worn a wedding-band throughout his travesty of a marriage, then determinedly put the woman who'd betrayed him and brought him such grief out of her mind.

As the car ate up the miles, she was perfectly content to sit back and watch the ease with which he maneuvered them through the various turnoffs toward the mountain town of Vail while he dealt with her son. The two of them conversed with a naturalness and camaraderie that some fathers and sons never achieved in a lifetime of living together.

If she was being really honest, she had to admit Jonah was more tolerant of Brody's precociousness than Rich had been, more willing to listen to him and give thoughtful answers.

Sarah couldn't explain why that should be, but, for just a little while, it didn't matter. The respite from having to be all things to Brody was rejuvenating. Not since Rich's last leave had she known this kind of freedom. Lulled into a kind of twilight slumber, because she hadn't slept all that well the night before, she rested her head against the window and closed her eyes.

She imagined that they'd been on the road about a half-hour when she heard Brody's stomach growl. She sat up with a start, shocked that anything could sound that loud. She and Brody broke into laughter at the same time that a deep chuckle rumbled out of Jonah. As she turned her head in her son's direction she encountered Jonah's smiling countenance, something she'd never seen before.

For an infinitesimal moment their eyes held. Her heart tumbled over and over itself as she drowned in the heady sensation.

Laughter made him look several years younger, transforming him from the angry, forbidding person of an hour ago into the most devastatingly handsome man she'd ever met in her life. She could hardly breathe.

'Jonah? Can we stop and get something to eat? I'm hungry.'

Like pricking a balloon, Brody's voice dispelled the intangible aura that had made her feel a momentary closeness to Jonah. She looked away, embarrassed to have been caught feasting her eyes on him.

'So am I,' he murmured, in a voice that sounded deeper and huskier than usual. 'Starving, in fact,' she heard him say beneath his breath.

Something in the way he said the words sent a tremor through every cell of her body. Her hands gripped the sides of the seat, trying to quell the frantic beating of her heart.

'At the next turnoff, we'll pick up some hamburgers and shakes. That ought to hold us until we reach the spot I have in mind.'

'Are we all going to sleep in the same tent?' Brody finally asked the question foremost on Sarah's mind.

'That's the main idea. Can you think of a better way to stay cozy and warm?'

Sarah almost felt smothered by the heat pouring off her sensitized body. It was entirely possible she was running a fever.

'Nope. Besides, Mom might get scared if she had to sleep alone.'

'There's no chance of that tonight.'

CHAPTER SEVEN

LONG before they'd reached their destination in the mountains above Vail, the sun had slipped below the horizon, forcing Jonah to turn on the car heater.

'Aren't we going to camp here?' Brody questioned as they passed the sign for the Gore Creek campgrounds.

Jonah shook his head. 'No. We've got to climb another three thousand feet.'

'How come?'

'You'll find out after we get there,' Jonah said in a mysterious tone guaranteed to whet Brody's insatiable curiosity.

'Is it a surprise?'

'That's right.'

'Yippee!'

Sarah didn't know if she was as enthusiastic. How easy it had been to assure Jonah that she was prepared to withstand the elements in order to come with him. When they'd left Denver, the temperature had been hovering around ninety degrees.

But it was quite another matter to be as brave at eleven thousand feet above sea level, where the air was not only thin, but freezing cold. Already she could see snow on the peaks.

Jonah must have been here before, because he knew exactly which winding mountain road to take. Eventually it brought them to a rolling alpine meadow surrounded by lofty mountain peaks rising to a height of fourteen thousand feet or more.

They'd driven above timber line, away from all signs of civilization. As far as Sarah was concerned, they'd reached the top of the world.

No longer resembling a carpet of flowers, the tiny broadleaf plants and vegetation had already turned to fall colors of brown and gold.

Sarah had never been to such an isolated spot before, but oddly enough she didn't feel nervous or frightened in such primitive grandeur. Jonah was the kind of man to inspire confidence. He would always be able to take care of himself and anyone else, which was why she and Brody felt totally secure.

He pulled the car off the track into the meadow, but in order to keep the heater running, he didn't turn off the motor. 'Both of you stay inside until I get you more clothes to put on.'

Brody made a little sound of excitement and turned around on his knees to watch Jonah through the rear window. He couldn't stay still and kept bouncing up and down, eager to get out of the car and join him. Sarah heard her son's deep sigh. 'I want him to be my teacher forever.'

His fervent wish didn't surprise her. 'You know what Jonah said,' she reminded him quietly. 'He'll only be here till Christmas. Then he has to go back to California.'

'Why?'

'Because that's his home. He's the head of a big company that makes programs for computers. There are lots of people depending on him.'

'But nobody wants Mrs Ruff to come back. If Jonah leaves, none of us are going to go to school anymore.'

She didn't know whether to laugh or cry, and wished the subject had never come up. 'Brody—let's not worry about that right now. Why don't we enjoy our campout and be thankful for the opportunity? In a minute, Jonah will need help. Do you remember how to erect his tent?'

'Sure. It's easy.'

She supposed that was true, but her main concern lay in the fact that it was fairly small. Three people would fill it completely. When she recalled the feel of Jonah's hair sifting through her fingers, the contours of his hard jaw, she started to tremble. Brody would have to sleep between them.

As if he'd known she'd been thinking about him, Jonah tapped on her window. With the suffocating feeling still in her chest, she opened the door and tried not to stare at the disturbingly attractive picture he made wearing a lined, weather-worn Levi jacket with the collar turned up against the rugged lines and angles of his arresting face.

His Levis molded to his powerful legs and thighs, accentuating his blatant masculinity. She felt a weakness in her lower limbs just being near him.

'Here's a couple of old parkas. Brody can pull on the bottoms to my ski underwear and you can wear a pair of my sweats.'

'Thank you,' she whispered shakily as he thrust the clothes in her arms, avoiding his eyes because it was getting harder and harder to remain detached around him.

By the time she'd made a knot in the elastic band of the ski underwear encircling Brody's slim waist, and had stepped into Jonah's navy sweats, he'd already lighted a lantern and had started putting up the tent.

Needing to keep moving to ward off the cold, Sarah and Brody assisted him, then helped him unload the rest of the gear from the car.

To Brody's delight, it was like reaching into Mary Poppins' magic bag. They kept pulling things out, everything from a fold-up camping table and chairs to coolers and a Coleman stove.

Brody looked all around him. 'How are we going to build a fire? There aren't any trees.'

'We can camp wherever we want up here, as long as we don't make a fire.'

'But, Jonah? How are we going to keep warm?'

'With these.' He pulled out a couple of propane heaters. 'Once we light them inside the tent, we'll be warm as a batch of bunnies in a rabbit hole.'

Brody's spontaneous laughter touched her heart. He was in ecstasy and kept up a running commentary, wanting to know how to turn them on. His questions helped Sarah to remain in the background, where she could listen and learn from Jonah, but Brody's natural interest in everything, plus his animation, probably drove Jonah to distraction.

Yet every time Sarah glimpsed a look at him when she thought he wasn't watching, she detected a faint half-smile on his lips and knew his affection for Brody was genuine. When his exuberance threatened to get out of control, Jonah used firmness and logic to guide him back without Brody being aware of it.

'Now for the surprise,' Jonah finally announced, lifting out a tripod and an expensive-looking case from the trunk.

'What is it?'

'Open it very carefully and you'll find out.' He set it on the ground for Brody, who immediately undid the snaps.

After some difficulty he cried. 'A *telescope*! Mom——'

'Tonight we're going to see sights you've never even dreamed of.'

He and Brody walked a few hundred yards away from the tent. If such a thing was possible, his excitement seemed to suppress Brody's, infecting Sarah, who felt little chills of anticipation race up and down her spine.

Brody wanted to forgo everything so he could peek through the lens. Sarah couldn't blame him, not since she was anxious to do the same thing.

'First we have to set up the cooking tent and eat our dinner.'

'A cooking tent?' Brody exclaimed in surprise.

Jonah quirked an eyebrow. 'Can you feel the wind?' Brody nodded. 'It's starting to pick up. If your mother doesn't have protection, her bare feet will turn to ice before she can fix our food.'

His eyes gleamed with a devilish light as they sought hers. The glow from the lantern cast his features into stark relief, once more impressing her with his arresting male beauty.

'How about it, Sarah?'

Her eyes narrowed in unknowing provocation. 'So now I'm going to have to pay.'

Something flickered in the dark recesses of his eyes. 'After what you pulled this afternoon, did you honestly think you wouldn't?'

The barest suggestion of more retribution to come laced his low, husky rejoinder, heightening her anxiety while at the same time reducing her to a quivering lump of inexplicable longings.

'Can we set up the tent now?' Brody interjected impatiently, bringing Sarah out of her tortured thoughts.

'So be it, Brody,' Jonah said, with more presence of mind than she could muster. 'Let's place it behind the other tent for protection from the wind.'

As they walked away Sarah heard, 'It's going to take forever until we get to look through the telescope.'

'Don't be so sure. Let's see who can do their side the fastest.'

Sarah smiled at the way Jonah handled Brody without making outright judgements or demands. There was no question in her mind that, if required, Brody would follow Jonah to the ends of the earth. He was her son's own personal guru.

Within minutes they had erected the tent, one that looked as if it had been used many times, yet was clean and large enough to hold all their food, tables and chairs, and cooking gear.

Throughout the course of the evening, Sarah stood next to the heater while she prepared the potatoes and onions and watched over the succulent T-bone steaks cooking on the grill. Every so often she stole a glance out the little window at the two of them huddled in the open meadow.

Jonah had gone down on his haunches to assemble the telescope to the tripod. Brody was at eye-level with him, and at one point he must have said something amusing because Jonah suddenly threw his head back and laughed. It was the rich kind of laughter that rang in the biting fall night air. The happy sound thrilled her, but it also brought a huge lump to her throat.

He was a natural teacher, a natural everything—how ironic that there could be so many undeserving fathers in the world, yet Jonah, of all people, wasn't able to have a child of his own. The horrid cliché that life wasn't fair seemed particularly applicable in Jonah's case.

While her gaze stretched across the high meadow, where the mountains formed a silhouette in the darkness, she couldn't help but wonder what kind of a woman would have put her marriage to Jonah in jeopardy. Sarah surmised that his wife had to have been mentally unstable to risk losing anyone as remarkable. It didn't make sense.

Sarah couldn't think of another person who came close to being his equal. No man of her acquaintance compared to him in any way, shape or form.

As the ramifications of that earthshaking discovery began to take root inside her she swayed slightly from the impact, and felt the blood drain out of her face.

Thank heavens Brody and Jonah were too far away to witness her moment of truth.

She shut off the propane stove, then shouted, 'Come and get it!' While she waited for them, she put the food on the small, square-shaped metal camp table.

Maybe it was the high altitude, but within minutes all three of them had assembled and began devouring their food as if they hadn't eaten for a week.

Brody gulped everything much too fast because he was so anxious to get back to the telescope. In between bites he explained that it had a fourteen-inch reflector mirror which Jonah said would make everything so much clearer.

Naturally he would've purchased the best equipment, Sarah mused to herself, finding herself every bit as eager as Brody to sample its power.

She played hostess, but studiously avoided any physical contact with Jonah as she refilled his coffee-cup. If she kept her gaze focused on Brody, she hoped to make it through to bedtime without too much more emotional upheaval.

Except for the grill and cooking utensils, which needed to be washed, virtually everything else was disposable. Sarah expected to do the clean-up, but it was Jonah who volunteered to take over, assuring her that the only reason he was willing to pitch in was because her cooking had surpassed his expectations. The compliment shouldn't have pleased her so much.

Once the coolers containing the food and drinks had been put back in the trunk of the car, and the heater transferred to the other tent, Jonah pronounced them ready for the big event.

After bundling up in Jonah's parkas, they obeyed his suggestion that each of them bring a chair so they'd be able to relax while they took turns viewing the sky. Brody led the way, making whooping sounds. They reverberated through the atmosphere, which had grown colder due to the wind.

When they reached the telescope, Sarah watched in womanly fascination as Jonah straddled one leg of the tripod and zoomed in on a portion of sky to the southeast.

The muscles running up his calves and thighs looked whipcord-strong. Her mouth went dry as she imagined them entwined with her own.

'Okay, Brody. Stand on this chair and grab hold of my shoulders. Then you can look through the lens to your heart's content. What you'll be looking at is the planet Saturn. You remember that we talked about it in class.'

A kind of joyous bark escaped Brody's lips as Jonah swung him from the ground with effortless grace. When she saw her son's small hands slide up Jonah's broad back and cling to him while he put his eye to the glass, she let out an involuntary moan, envying him that closeness.

After a palpable silence he shouted, 'Mom—wait till you see *this*! It has *rings*! It's awesome!'

On some level she registered Brody's wondering outburst, but she was too overwhelmed by the force of her own raw emotions to respond with any coherence.

Chastising herself for being so out of control, she deliberately gazed upward, pleading silently for release from Jonah's dominating presence and her intense attraction to him. Only she wasn't prepared to be swallowed up in something which seemed to be part of the magic of the night.

'Oh, Jonah . . .' She cried out from her soul, just as Brody had done, and got to her feet, transfixed by the matchless glory of the heavens.

Against a backdrop of the blackest velvet, an infinity of glittering stars looked like shattered crystal flung every which way, filling the tiniest centimeter of space as far and as deep as the eye could see.

She put up her hands to keep her long black hair from blowing in her face and turned in all directions, gasping with incredulity. 'I've never seen anything so beautiful in my life.'

Jonah looked back over his shoulder, his shuttered gaze finding hers. 'I agree,' came the low, oddly thick-sounding response, reminding her of their conversation in the tent on Jeff's lawn.

Was it only last night?

A lifetime seemed to have passed by since then.

Because everything has changed, her pounding heart told her. Because you've fallen hopelessly in love with him.

Her eyes closed tightly with the strength of her feelings. From the first moment he'd appeared at her condo, even before he'd been drenched to the skin covering his powerful body, she'd known she was in trouble.

Her relationship with Rich had been so different. Friendship had preceded their love, with many letters passing back and forth while he was at sea.

This cataclysm of feeling she'd experienced from the very second she'd opened the door to Jonah had been so frightening in its intensity that she'd done everything possible to repress it.

Out of self-preservation, she'd retaliated with anger, not knowing how else to combat the sensation of helplessness he'd engendered by simply being himself.

Sarah had had no idea she could ever love another man again, let alone feel as if she'd just discovered the meaning of the word.

When she'd least expected it, love had come to her full-blown—heady, passionate, all-consuming.

Standing next to him, as she was now, created an inferno of want and need that turned her inside-out and made her yearn to know his possession.

'Sarah?' She heard him call her name in a quiet, almost unrecognizable voice.

'Wh-What?' she answered shakily, terrified to turn around and allow him to discern her secret. Dear God. She didn't dare let him know how she felt. He could never find out!

Though she knew he wasn't indifferent to her, she also recognized that Brody had been the catalyst which had forced their paths to cross. Otherwise they wouldn't be here now.

What haunted her most was the fact that Jonah had lived through a disastrous marriage which had taught him the pain of a woman's treachery. Such an exceptional man might never love again. And, even if he did, he'd be slow to act upon it. Sarah suffered the growing suspicion that she'd never live enough years for that to happen.

'I asked if you'd like to look through the lens now.'

Her senses reeled. 'In a minute. Right now I'm fascinated with all the shooting stars.' She grasped at the first plausible excuse available to her.

'I admit there's more activity than usual. Those long streaks across the sky are probably the last remnants of the Perseus meteor shower.'

She finally found the strength to turn in his direction. 'How do you know so much about it?'

'It's been a hobby of mine as long as I can remember. I'd always intended to be an astronomer, but when my business took off unexpectedly, I had to put my studies on hold.'

'Mom—come on and look!' Brody spoke up, jarring her out of another reverie. Everything that Jonah said or did intrigued her and increased her need to know more.

After Brody jumped off the chair, Jonah set it aside to make room for her. But, to her consternation, he remained standing next to her so their arms brushed against each other as she stepped up to the glass.

Her whole body trembling, she tried to pretend that he wasn't there, that she couldn't hear him breathing or feel the warmth from his body.

Her first look at Saturn didn't seem real. She could actually see the division between the two brightest rings. 'How incredible. I can't believe what I'm seeing. Brody, honey—this is fantastic!'

With a stealth she could scarcely credit, Jonah moved behind her. The blood started pounding in her ears. 'Now try this.'

With his arms encircling her, he moved the scope to a different position, lowering his head to site in the portion of sky he wanted her to see. The subtle scent of the soap he used assailed her nostrils. In the process, the side of his face inadvertently rubbed against hers, coaxing a tiny gasp from her throat.

Once more she put her eye to the glass, unable to stop shaking. Maybe he would blame the chilling night air for her palsy-like condition.

Again, Sarah found the view absolutely astounding. 'This is probably the most exciting thing I've ever done.'

There was a smile in Jonah's voice when he said, 'You're looking at Jupiter. How many moons can you see?'

'I want to look,' Brody cried out.

'All in good time. Let's let your mother have her turn.'

Feeling an elation she'd never known before, she started to count. 'I think I can spot four of them. This telescope makes everything so crisp and clear. I had no idea . . .'

'Let me make one more adjustment and you can look at Mars.'

Afraid to relax, she stood perfectly still while his strong arms reached around her yet a second time, bringing his hard, muscled legs in direct contact with the backs of hers.

'There. Now try,' he murmured, his breath like a caress against her hot cheek.

Dizzy from the sensation, she realized that she couldn't stay this close to him and function with any coherence. In a quavering voice she said, 'I—I can see the reddish tinge I've always heard about. Come here, Brody.'

Out of desperation, she reached for her son and picked him up in her arms, not the least ashamed to use him as a shield against Jonah's magnetism. Besides, her son's wiry body was warm and she needed his heat.

For the next little while she clung to Brody like a refuge, while he viewed everything from the Pegasus and Cassiopeia constellations to the Andromeda.

'Wow! It looks like a cotton-ball.'

Jonah chuckled deep in his throat, sending a dart of awareness to every nerve-ending in her body. He hadn't moved from his stance behind her. 'That's a perfect description, Brody. You're eyeing the Andromeda Galaxy. It's twenty thousand light-years away.'

Sarah shook her head. 'I can't comprehend that.'

'Nor can I,' came the deep voice over her shoulder.

'Is that where heaven is, Jonah?' asked Brody.

There was a perceptible silence. Then, 'Yes. I believe it is.'

'Dad's in heaven. Do you think he could see us if he had a telescope?'

'Where he is, he doesn't need one,' Jonah answered in a thick-toned voice. 'He can see you whenever he wants.'

Jonah's tender sensitivity brought unbidden tears to Sarah's eyes. She fought to keep them from spilling down her cheeks.

'Can we come up here again so I can see where he lives?'

'As often as your mother says it's all right.'

Suddenly Brody twisted around, a look of adoration in his incandescent blue eyes. 'I love you, Jonah.'

The honest, open avowal was too much for Sarah, whose arms tightened around Brody as Jonah tousled her son's dark hair. 'I love you, too, sport.'

Stifling a moan, she said, 'I think it's too cold to stay out here any longer, honey.'

'But I don't want to go to bed yet.'

'Your mother's right, Brody. There'll be other nights.'

'Okay,' he muttered a reluctant noise of consent.

Sarah whispered in his ear, 'Is that any way to talk after everything Jonah has done for us? He didn't have to bring us up here, you know. You need to thank him.'

Brody was immediately contrite, and wriggled to the ground. He looked up at Jonah. 'Thanks for letting us come and look through your telescope. When I grow up I want to be just like you.'

Jonah had started disassembling his equipment, but when he heard those words he paused in the action of putting the scope back in its case.

'That's the greatest compliment I've ever been paid,' he said in quiet tones, 'but I can tell you right now that all you have to do is continue to be yourself and you'll grow into a fine man just like your father.'

Brody cocked his head. Through the mist veiling her eyes Sarah could see his confusion. 'But you never met my dad.'

Jonah's mouth curved into a thoughtful half-smile.

'That's true, but I've met you, haven't I? There's an old saying, "like father, like son".'

He pondered Jonah's comment for a minute, then said, 'When you have a son, I bet he'll be tall. And smart!'

Sarah didn't dare look at Jonah, for fear she'd see pain in his eyes, and reached abruptly for Brody's hand. 'Come on, honey. I'm freezing.'

She pulled him toward the car, parked some distance from their camp. Since there was no restroom available, they'd have to make do a little ways behind it.

In a few minutes they'd returned to their tent, whose interior, though dark, was comfortably warm and inviting from the heater.

Anxious to be in bed before Jonah entered, Sarah helped Brody shed his parka, then took off her own. She spread them out over the top of the double sleeping-bag Jonah had insisted they use. His foam rubber pad and quilts lay cross-wise in front of the opening.

'Do you want to hand me your sandals?'

Once she'd put their shoes against the wall of the tent, she crawled under the covers. After turning on her side and shaping the pillow to her liking, she drew Brody into her arms.

His little back nestled against her chest and stomach. 'Mom . . . This was the best time of my whole life.'

She inhaled deeply. 'I'm glad.'

'I thought you'd be mad,' he said in a small, timid voice.

Frowning, she lifted her head and stroked the hair on his forehead. 'Mad? Why would you think that?'

'Because I told Jonah I loved him. I was afraid it would make you cry.'

She swallowed hard. 'I can see why you love Jonah. He's a wonderful man and he's brought you a great deal of happiness. Since you're the most important person in my life, that makes me happy, not sad.'

Brody rolled over so he was facing her. 'Do you mean it?'

'Yes, honey. I know I used to cry a lot, mostly because I love you so much. I was afraid I couldn't be as good a mother to you as you needed.'

'You were crying 'cause you were afraid?' he asked in childish amazement.

'Yes.'

'Don't ever be afraid, Mom. You're the best.' He gave her a hug and a kiss.

She hugged him back, ruffling his hair. 'I'm not afraid. Not anymore.'

It was true.

Jonah's advent into their lives had caused a great change to come over her. She had no idea what lay in their future, but one thing was certain. She'd come a long way out of yesterday, and had finally put the past behind her.

'Goodnight, Mom.'

'Goodnight, honey.'

The day had been a big one for Brody. It didn't surprise her that he fell asleep almost immediately. The combination of so much excitement and the high altitude had forced him to succumb without any inducement on her part.

For a long time she lay there, listening to the mournful sound of the wind as it blew around the tent. She didn't know if Jonah's absence was deliberate or not. If he was in deep pain, he'd never allow her to see it, let alone try to ease it.

Her thoughts flashed back to the things he'd told her about his wife, awful things that would leave scars. Sarah grew restless and turned away from Brody.

After the way she'd treated Jonah since their first meeting, he'd look with skepticism at any attempt on her part to make amends for her former hostility.

He'd already warned her that he didn't want her pity. That was how he'd construe any future gestures of conciliation. Certainly that was how he'd view today's outing, but, to spare Brody's feelings, he'd gone along with her ploy.

A new terror filled her heart, because she realized Jonah would never allow her to get away with it a second time.

She buried her wet face in the pillow and tried to stifle the sound. In no circumstances did she want Brody to wake up. Otherwise he'd discover that she couldn't keep her promise not to cry, not even for one night.

CHAPTER EIGHT

'MOM?' Brody had just drained his glass of milk. Some of the residue remained on his upper lip. 'Is Jonah going to drive us to the game today?'

Sarah eyed her son balefully. 'I think that's about the tenth time you've asked me that question. The answer is, no. We're all going to ride the bus to the stadium,' she explained in her brightest voice to mask the hurt that a week of virtual silence on Jonah's part since their campout in the mountains had wrought.

She never had heard him come to bed that night, and, when she and Brody had awakened the next morning, he had already started breakfast in the cooking tent.

On the surface, everything had seemed perfectly normal and pleasant, because Jonah would never have done anything to disturb Brody's peace of mind. But, on the drive home, Sarah had sensed Jonah's emotional withdrawal from her.

When he'd dropped them off at the back door of the condo, there'd been no offer of a follow-up outing, only a casual reminder that Sarah would be needed to help chaperon the kids at the game scheduled for Friday.

Oblivious to Sarah's pain, a beaming Brody went to school the next day, and all had gone along smoothly. But right now he couldn't hide his disappointment that he wouldn't be getting preferential treatment by going to the game in Jonah's car.

'Remember what Jonah told you on the way home from Vail?' She cleared away the rest of the lunch dishes and loaded them in the dishwasher. 'You can't let the other kids know you've been camping with him. It isn't fair to them. Think how bad you'd feel, how left out, if you saw Jeff riding in Jonah's car when the rest of you weren't invited.'

'I guess so,' he muttered, his head bowed forlornly. 'Can I go camping with him next weekend?'

Her heart leaped in her throat. 'Did he ask you?'

'No.'

His response shouldn't have caused her spirits to take such a downward spiral. 'I suppose that's because the weather has turned cold. Halloween's going to be here pretty soon, which means there's more snow in the mountains. It's too cold to camp up there again until next spring.'

'Next spring?' He looked horrified.

'I'm not saying we couldn't go to Vail for the day, but the road up to the meadow where we camped is probably impassable already.'

'Oh, heck.'

'Hey—I don't like to hear that, not when Jonah has arranged for you to see a football game. Now run and get your parka and we'll drive over to school.'

'I'm going to sit by him at the game. Maybe he'll ask me to go camping with him then,' he called from the hallway.

Sarah couldn't bring herself to make a comment. She had the distinct impression that, since their night in the mountains, Jonah had decided to low-key his relationship with Brody. Though he'd mentioned something about playing ping-pong with him, that plan had never materialized.

After her son's demonstration of love, which had gone far beyond the bounds of hero-worship, Jonah must have been shocked. Though he hadn't taken her previous warnings seriously, he now knew he was treading in uncharted waters. The time would soon come when he'd have to turn over the class to Mrs Ruff and go back to California.

In his wisdom, he had chosen to start letting Brody down gently. Sarah could find no fault with his tactics, but she didn't know what to do about her own tortured state of mind.

Since their return from Vail she'd felt exceptionally emotional and nervy. She hadn't been sleeping well. Every time the phone rang, or the front doorbell sounded, her heart practically jumped out of its cavity, anticipating Jonah's face or voice. She'd been counting the hours until they met at the bus.

In her chaotic state she'd changed outfits four times, finally deciding on jeans and a deep red wool sweater which she wore with a waist-fitting leather jacket. The dark brown crushed suede material matched her boots and would keep her warm.

She didn't apply make-up except for lipstick. She was feverish with excitement and anxiety, and her skin held a natural blush stain. As for her heavily lashed blue eyes and arched brows, whose black color matched her shoulder-length hair, they required no artifice.

'Come on, Brody. We've got to get there before the others.'

'I can't find my Chargers hat.'

'It's right here on the kitchen table where you left it.' Like his mom, Brody was showing all the tell-tale signs of jittery excitement because they'd be spending the rest of the day with a man who'd come to mean everything to them.

Five minutes later, Sarah pulled the car into the parking lot of the school where she could see the district bus waiting.

Gratified to have arrived ahead of everyone else, she got out and locked the doors while Brody ran over to talk to the driver.

It was a typical fall day with a marginal bite in the air; the sun was doing its best to pierce the light cloud cover. In Sarah's opinion, it was perfect football weather. The kids would be able to last all four quarters without freezing to death.

Her eyes darted repeatedly to the street, watching for the Jaguar. One week's abstinence had felt like a year.

But she was destined to be disappointed when every color car but green pulled into the parking lot, depositing shrieking, euphoric children. There was no sign of Lynette, who was also supposed to be helping.

Of necessity, Sarah chatted with each of the parents, assuring them she'd watch over things and make sure all went well.

Jeff's parents drove in at the last minute and issued an invitation to Brody to come over to their house after the ball-game for pizza. They were going to show some Disney videos, and they asked Sarah to join in.

She accepted for both of them, but had to pretend to be enthused, because a part of her was hoping the evening might turn out differently.

Heavens, she was worse than Brody, because she had every intention of spending it with Jonah. Since last night she'd been plotting how to accomplish that feat without him accusing her of feeling sorry for him.

A glance at her watch told her they'd better be leaving for the stadium in a few minutes. She couldn't understand Lynette being so late.

Where was Jonah?

It wasn't like him not to show up on time for something this important, especially when he'd accomplished the impossible by arranging an outing every parent in the school would have given anything to go on.

Brody jumped off the bottom step of the bus and raced up to her, wearing a look of concern on his expressive face. 'Mom? Do you want me to run to Jonah's and get him?'

'No, honey. He'll be here.'

'Maybe his car doesn't work.'

'If that was the case, he'd jog over...' Her voice trailed as she spied Lynette's white Ford in the distance.

Gratified she'd finally come, because Sarah didn't want the whole weight of the outing on her shoulders, she and Brody walked over to the red-headed mother, who took her time getting out of the car.

Talia bounced out her side and ran over to the bus, shouting to the kids, 'Jonah's not coming. He's sick.'

Schooling her features to show no emotion, Sarah cast a glance at her son, who had raced after Talia in a panic.

'Is that true?' Sarah questioned the younger woman, so devastated by the news she could hardly bear it. 'Is Jonah too ill to go with us?'

'Yes.' The younger woman nodded. 'He's had a bad cold all week, but last night I noticed it had gone into his chest and was much worse. He went over to emergency this morning for an injection of some kind and has been ordered to bed. I did what I could to make him comfortable. That's why I'm late. He gave me the tickets and all the instructions. Shall we go?'

Without waiting for a reply, she walked off.

Sarah trembled with the gamut of emotions, ranging from stabbing jealousy over this woman's privileged place in Jonah's life to stark fear for his physical well-being.

Calling upon every bit of strength and willpower she possessed, Sarah carried on for the rest of the day as if Jonah's absence didn't matter. She had to put on the performance of her life—not only for Brody, whose day had been robbed of joy, but for the other children, who adored their teacher and didn't want to go anywhere without him.

There were very few people in the world Sarah disliked. But, try as she might, she couldn't warm to Lynette, who up to this time had done little if nothing to help, and now, suddenly, had decided to take charge.

Throughout the football game, dominated and won by the Broncos—much to Brody's and Sarah's disappointment—Lynette found several opportunities to let Sarah know that she enjoyed a close relationship with Jonah which gave her certain rights. But the *coup de grâce* came when she intimated that she'd probably be spending Thanksgiving in San Diego with him.

With shattered expectations, and such a drastic change in circumstances, Sarah found herself grateful for the invitation to spend the evening at Jeff's house. Both she and Brody needed to stay involved and occupied so they wouldn't dwell on the one person Sarah refused to discuss with Brody as long as there were other people around.

By the end of the night she had decided it would be a good idea to ask Jeff to sleep over at their house. She waited until the last film finished before broaching the subject, which was met with enthusiasm by everyone. All except for Brody, who had a hard time drumming up any excitement now that his day had been ruined.

But Sarah knew herself too well. She was in no shape to deal with his pain right now, not when she was wrestling with new agonies brought on by the comments which Lynette had seemed to enjoy dropping throughout the game.

It wasn't so much that Sarah considered Lynette a serious threat—Sarah had a hunch that the other woman tended to exaggerate to make herself feel important. What hurt Sarah most was the fact that Jonah would deliberately turn to someone else rather than ask her for any help, especially when he only lived two doors away from their condo.

In a way, she felt responsible for his flu. After all, she'd forced herself on him so he'd take her and Brody to the mountains. Because of her selfishness he'd had to give up his sleeping-bag, which had meant trying to stay warm under a couple of inadequate quilts.

Once the heater had been shut off for the night, the temperature had plummeted, but Jonah had never said a word about his own discomfort.

By the time she'd gone home with the boys and settled them down for the night, she was worried enough about Jonah to call him and see if there was anything she could do for him.

But, after picking up the receiver, she thought the better of it and put it down again, unable to find the courage. She supposed it was possible that Lynette could be with him. The last thing Sarah wanted was to be caught phoning Jonah and having to explain anything to the other woman.

It was entirely possible he'd encouraged Lynette to go over there after the game, to give him a rundown on the afternoon's activities. Sarah didn't want to admit that there might be other reasons more intimate and personal for Jonah to desire the redhead's company.

Tortured by certain pictures that filled her mind, Sarah paced the kitchen floor. The only way to find out if he was alone was to make a quick run to his condo. But if she did that she'd have to tell the boys, in case they got up to look for her and found the place empty.

She supposed she could wait another half-hour, until she was certain they were in a sound sleep.

Deciding she'd go mad if she watched the clock, she went into the dining-room and dug into one of the cases she'd been working on. No sooner had she started recording information than Brody wandered in the room, his hair sticking out in several directions.

'Brody?' Sarah groaned, afraid of what was coming. 'What are you doing up, honey? I thought you were asleep.'

'Talia said if Jonah gets pneumonia, he might die.'

Before Rich's death, she might have considered her son's fears trivial and brushed them off. But, thanks to Jonah's insight, she now knew to take his worries seriously. In truth, anxiety over the state of Jonah's condition had been eating her alive as well.

Making a decision, she put her pen down and got to her feet. 'I'll tell you what. You lock the door after me, and I'll run across to his condo to see if he needs anything.'

'Can't I come?'

'No. You have to stay with Jeff, in case he wakes up. Okay? I'll hurry right back.'

'Okay. Can I turn on the TV while I wait for you?'

Recognizing he'd never go to sleep until he'd been reassured, Sarah nodded. 'Just not too loud.'

Because Lynette would park in front of Jonah's condo, where there were streetlights and spaces to park, Sarah left by the front door.

Because it was only ten o'clock, she assumed that if Jonah was alone he might not be asleep yet, unless of course his doctor had prescribed medication which had made him drowsy.

To her great relief, when she rounded the curve and stepped beyond a clump of pines, Lynette's car was nowhere in sight. As for Jonah's condo, everything looked dark. If he was trying to sleep, then he wouldn't appreciate being awakened.

But the need to see for herself that he was all right warred with caution, and won out. Quickly, before she lost her nerve, she dashed up the front porch and rang the buzzer.

When there was no response, she tried the knob. It didn't give.

Perspiration broke out on her brow. What if he needed help and couldn't make it to the door?

No longer worried about what was right or wrong, she ran around to the back, noting that his car was in its stall. Without hesitation she rang the buzzer. Still no response. She tried the knob. It wouldn't turn.

Compelled by an urgency stronger than anything she'd known before, she knocked on the door several times. 'Jonah? Are you there? Can you at least tell me if yo——?'

But she never finished her question, because the door suddenly opened and he stood in the aperture, dressed in nothing more than a pair of shorts which rode dangerously low on his hips. The light from the back of the carport cast his face in shadow. Even so she thought she detected a slight flush on his hard-boned cheeks.

'What do you want?' came a deep, rasping voice that was virtually unrecognizable.

'I—I don't want anything,' she defended, wounded to the quick by his terse question. 'I came to see if you needed help.'

His mouth tautened to a pencil-thin line. 'I've received a surfeit of unsolicited help already.'

If by that comment he meant Lynette, then it didn't look as if the other woman's attention had been well-received either, which filled Sarah with unholy joy. But that emotion was shortlived when she saw him sway and clutch the edge of the door with both hands for support.

Some of his hair was damp and swirled in tendrils around his forehead and nape. His unshaven jaw added to the look of dishevelment brought about by his illness.

'You have a bad fever.' She tried to keep the alarm out of her voice. 'I can feel the heat coming off your body and see it in your face. Maybe you should go to the hospital. I'll drive you there.'

'For the love of God—— Don't you know when you're n-not wanted?' His speech sounded slurred. 'G-Go home and leave me alone.'

He tried to push the door shut, but she wouldn't let him. Though his words were meant to drive her away, he'd delivered them in such a strained voice that she knew he was about ready to pass out on her.

Operating on sheer instinct, Sarah moved swiftly inside and lifted one of his arms around her shoulders. Gripping his hand with hers, she wrapped her free arm around his lean waist. 'Hold on tight, Jonah. I'm going to help you to your bed.'

His body was too hot. Once Brody had had a fever like this and she'd brought it down with cold, wet bathtowels and aspirin.

Unlike her son, however, Jonah cursed incoherently all the way through the kitchen and down the hall, but had lost too much strength to fight her.

She led him to the first bedroom, which turned out to be the one he used, if the tumble of sheets and bedding was any indication.

With a simple nudge, he fell back against the mattress. She lifted his legs on to the king-sized bed, then raced to the bathroom to see what medicine she could find.

To her everlasting relief she found paracetanol in the cabinet. After filling a glass with water, she took two pills in to him and forced him to swallow them. He fought her every step of the way, but, because he was almost delirious, it was like dealing with an oversized baby.

Once that was accomplished, she rushed back to the bathroom and soaked a couple of large bathtowels in cold water. When she'd wrung them out enough to keep them from dripping all over the carpet, she carried them into the bedroom, where Jonah stirred restlessly and mumbled nonsensical words.

As she'd done with Brody, she laid one towel lengthwise from his face to his chest, the other on top of his thighs and lower limbs.

Jonah groaned in protest at the shock, but she continued to press the cool toweling into his hot skin to soak up the heat. Sitting at his side, she leaned over and began to bathe his face with the top edge of the towel, squeezing cool moisture over his forehead and cheeks, on to his parched lips.

'I have to do this, my darling,' she murmured tenderly, brushing her lips against his forehead. 'Forgive me.'

Each time a towel lost its chill, she took it back to the bathroom and repeated the process, allowing the cold water to work its magic over every exposed part of his body, which had become as precious to her as Brody's.

Within a half-hour he was definitely cooler and had fallen into a light sleep. She kept the towels draped over him and reached for the phone on the bedside table to call Patsy, unaware until now that the T-shirt she'd changed into after the game was sopping wet too.

Speaking in hushed tones, she explained what had happened. Patsy offered to go over to the condo and stay with the children for the rest of the night. Sarah thanked her profusely, then got hold of Brody who was waiting for her.

'Is Jonah going to be all right?' he asked anxiously.

'Yes. He'll be fine, but I have to stay with him till I know he's feeling better. Jeff's mom will be over in a few minutes. Okay?'

'Why can't I see Jonah now?'

'Because he's asleep.'

'Okay,' he mumbled.

'Listen for Patsy, and I'll see you later. Love you.'

'Love you, too. Mom?'

'Yes?'

'Tell Jonah I love him.'

Her eyes smarted. 'I will. Goodnight, honey.'

She put the receiver back on the hook, relieved she didn't have to worry about the boys and could give all of her attention to Jonah for the rest of the night.

Another trip to the bathroom with the towels and she was satisfied that, at least for the present, the combination of pills and cold water had abated the fever.

Leaving the large towels in the tub, she took a hand-towel, then made a trip to the kitchen and wrapped up some ice in it.

After locking the back door, she returned to the bedroom and drew a sheet to his chin with its five o'clock shadow. Then she lay down next to him, propped herself on one elbow, and started to wipe his face gently.

The natural light from the moon spilled through the window and bathed the room with its glow, enough to discern his features. For the rest of the night she could drink her fill of his beloved face.

Slowly her eyes slid over the contours of his superb male physique. Never in her life had she seen such a man. He was absolutely perfect to her.

For a long time she fantasized about what it would be like to have the right to lie next to him like this always, to wake up to him every morning, to go to bed with him every night.

Little by little she relaxed and lowered her head on her arm, still continuing to keep his face cool with her free hand.

At some point her lids felt heavy. She fought to keep them open. If his fever spiked again, she needed to cool him down all over again...

'Brody——' she murmured, when she became cognizant of a weight across her stomach. Her hands moved to ease him off her and encountered a head of hair and shoulders that couldn't possibly belong to her son.

Her eyes flew open.

A strange man's bedroom greeted her vision before she remembered...

'*Jonah*,' she cried in heartfelt panic, because she'd fallen asleep when it was the last thing she'd wanted to do. By the light, she could tell it was morning.

At the sound of his name resounding in the room he stirred, and finally lifted his head from its soft resting place, still retaining his hold around her jean-clad hips.

'Sarah?' he blurted, as if he couldn't quite believe what he was seeing. He raised up a little more. 'It *is* you. I thought I'd been dreaming,' he said in a congested voice, several registers lower than normal.

Any other man in his condition would have looked a sight. But this was Jonah, and she loved him. He felt cool, which meant he'd gotten past the fever, thank heaven.

He shook his head as if to clear it, raking an unsteady hand through his dark blond hair. Though there were bruise-like smudges beneath his eyes, evidence of the illness racking his body last night, that frightened glaze had disappeared, leaving them a clear, dark velvety brown.

'How the hell did you get in here?'

Her heart skipped a beat. He was angry, which was the best of signs, though not necessarily for her. Last night's crisis had dictated her actions. But this morning he had recovered enough to make her face the consequences.

'You let me in,' she answered quietly, not daring to move. 'Don't you remember?'

He rubbed the hand not clasped around her body over the stubble of his jaw and chin. A sound of self-loathing escaped his throat.

Staring a little beyond her shoulder, he reached for the hand-towel she'd used to cool his face. The damp edges skimmed her cheeks as he held it up, evidence that the ice cubes had taken their time to melt.

His questioning eyes impaled hers. 'You sponged me down?' he whispered in disbelief.

She nodded. 'I had to. You were burning up.'

His brows met in a deep frown. 'How long have you been here?'

'Since ten-thirty last night. At the door you almost fainted on me, so I helped you in here. I gave you some paracetamol, then soaked you in wet towels until you fell asleep.'

'Good Lord.' She felt his body tense before he shoved a hand through his hair once more, obviously distraught. 'You said towels. Does that mean you nursed me all night?'

'I did what I could until I fell asleep.'

For the first time since she'd known him, his eyes fell away first. 'Sometimes I run a fever with a cold. It's a by-product of the injury to my spleen, but not as serious as you might suppose.' There was a tense pause. 'Did I say anything?' His voice grated.

Sarah eyed him lovingly. 'Nothing you could be put in jail for.'

His angry gaze swerved to hers. She had an idea he wasn't aware that his hand had tightened on her hip. 'Tell me the truth.'

Her eyes searched his for a timeless moment. 'What are you afraid of?'

She watched his throat work convulsively. 'Don't play games with me, Sarah.' He sounded in agony. 'I want to know what I said to get you in my bed.'

Without conscious thought she lifted her hand to his face, anxious to reassure him. 'You never said anything I could understand. I swear it.'

His jaw hardened and he trapped her hand in his solid grip. Strength had returned to his body in full force. 'Why did you come over here last night?'

She sucked in her breath. 'Why did you call Lynette instead of me when you realized you were too sick to go to the game with us?'

His eyes darkened. 'You know why.'

'Do I?' she fought back, desperate to disabuse him of any false notions he might be harboring where she was concerned. His first wife had done incredible damage to his psyche. Sarah had her work cut out for her.

'I knew how much Brody was counting on going to the game with me. If I'd dumped this in your lap, it's possible Brody might have refused to go and you would have had real trouble on your hands. It was easier to phone Talia's mother.'

'You made her day,' Sarah said, more sharply than she'd intended. 'But, as usual, you were right,' she murmured. 'You're always right where Brody is concerned. Though his heart wasn't in it, my son did go to the game. Everyone had a wonderful time, thanks to your generosity.'

A stillness came over Jonah. 'You still haven't answered my question.'

More than anything in the world, Sarah wanted to blurt out that she loved him, that he had become the whole meaning of her existence.

But she couldn't do that. He wasn't ready to hear it. He might never be ready...

CHAPTER NINE

'BRODY refused to go to bed until he knew you were all right. As soon as I told him you were sleeping soundly, but that I needed to stay with you, he was fine. Jeff's mother went over to sleep at my place for the rest of the night. The problem is, Talia said something about you getting pneumonia and dying. That was all my son needed to hear.'

He expelled a heavy sigh. 'There was never a question of my getting pneumonia or anything like it. That must have been a figment of Lynette's creative imagination. Because it helps keep up my resistance, I always go to the doctor for a shot of gamma when I sense a fever coming on. It doesn't happen more than once a year.'

Sarah tried to sit up, but he kept her pinned beneath him. 'I-It's my fault you got sick this time.' Tears filled her eyes, unbidden. 'I'm so sorry.'

His expression grew fierce. 'What in the hell are you talking about?'

'The night we camped out, you insisted that Brody and I use your sleeping-bag. Why didn't you tell me you were freezing? That you were susceptible?'

His eyelids drooped as he regarded her broodingly. 'Despite the fact that I caught a bug from one of my students in class, are you saying that you would have welcomed me inside that bag?' He asked the question in a slightly scathing tone.

She held her ground. 'I should think my presence in your bed all night long would make that question unnecessary.'

'For a grieving widow, I find your compassion for the poor unfortunates of this world rather astounding.' His scornful smile almost destroyed her. 'I wonder just how far you'd go in the name of comfort?'

'Don't Jonah——' she pleaded with him.

His eyes dilated. 'Don't what?' he mocked, slowly caressing her hip and slender waist with his hand, setting fire to her body with every sensuous stroke. 'Isn't this why you're here? To give hope and succor to the needy? In my case, to half a man?'

'Stop it,' she cried out aghast, feeling his pain, yet helpless to relieve it. As he drew closer she pounded on his shoulders with her fists, to no avail.

'The thing is, Sarah, though I'm not able to impregnate a woman, I *can* function as a man. At least I used to function as one,' he gibed in self-condemnation. 'Shall we find out if I'm still any good? Let me know later if I measure up in any way to your irreplaceable husband.' He spoke against her trembling lips.

Her puny attempts to fight him off proved futile against his male size and power. Once his mouth found hers, she was lost in a swirling maelstrom of ecstasy. Like her love for him, his full-blown passion assaulted and overwhelmed her senses, preventing her from holding back any secret part of herself.

Jonah didn't know his own strength. The demons driving him made him oblivious to everything but his need to find release from the pain. Sarah understood that pain.

Suddenly she wanted to immerse him in so much love he'd never feel the pain again.

Like a revelation it came to her that this was what she'd wanted from the very beginning. He was in her arms now, thrilling her, creating a mindless rapture which threatened to carry her away to a world where time and place were forgotten, where the only thing that remained was the burning desire to satisfy their mutual hunger.

No longer afraid to hold back, her mouth left his long enough to follow the path of her hands as they moved down his neck and over the broad shoulders she'd memorized last night. Though they hadn't exchanged wedding-vows, she was ready to worship him with her body.

Words would never do for a man like Jonah. Sarah would have to show him, over and over again, so that he finally believed in love again.

But, when her avid mouth sought his once more, he tried to withdraw, as if he sensed that she wasn't fighting him, that, indeed, she was showing a breathtaking response, giving him kiss for kiss, caress for caress.

When he groaned in protest, she called on hidden reserves and went after him, allowing him no respite, igniting new passions, determined not to let him go until he knew in the core of his being that she loved him.

'For the love of God, Sarah——' he cried on a tortured whisper, and shoved her away from him, getting unsteadily to his feet. He looked like a man who couldn't take anymore.

She lay there completely spent, drinking in draughts of air to fill her breathless lungs.

His eyes were mere slits of dark light. 'Why didn't you try to stop me?'

'Why didn't you finish what you started?' She answered his question with a question. 'I'm in agony.'

'You don't mean that.'

She raised herself to a sitting position, wishing she could shout out her love for him, but he'd never accept those words from her, at least not yet. Perhaps in time...

'I want you, Jonah,' she said in a low, tremulous voice, 'and I have proof that you want me.'

A forbidding mask wiped the expression from his face. 'You're missing a warm, live body in your bed.'

'Yes.' She nodded. 'Yours. I've been fantasizing about you since the night you came in from the rain.'

'I don't believe you.'

'If I had still been in mourning for my dead husband, do you honestly believe I would have invited you inside, let alone allowed you to wear his old robe?'

'Your son was responsible for everything that happened that night,' he fired back.

Sarah could see this was going to take time, and pushed the hair out of her face. She knew her cheeks were flushed, that her lips were slightly swollen from his lovemaking.

'Don't you dare blame the chemistry between us on Brody.'

'What chemistry?' he baited her.

'The chemistry John Marsden said was so thick he could cut it with a knife. I realize what he said wasn't very original, but he made his point just the same.

'Jonah—I could have left you standing out on the porch that night to wait for the taxi. I could have enrolled Brody in another elementary school altogether. For that matter, I could have moved to another part of Denver and sublet my sister's condo to strangers if I'd wanted to avoid you.'

'So what are you trying to say?' he bit out.

She took a shuddering breath. 'Simply that we're good together. All three of us.'

Taking the greatest calculated risk of her life, she ventured, 'H-How would you like to move in with Brody and me?'

Sarah had been raised in a very traditional home and had waited until her wedding-night to sleep with

Rich. But the situation couldn't be compared to anything remotely connected with Jonah.

The silence in the room was deafening. His pallor intensified, indicating that something earthshaking was going on inside of him.

'You could come and go to California as you please. Maybe you could use this condo for an office to work in after school and on weekends, then come home to Brody and me at night.' Her voice trembled. 'We would always be here for you.'

'You're not serious.'

'I'm very serious. You said it yourself. John didn't have a prayer with me because you're the only man I'm interested in.'

His hands went to his hips. 'What would you tell Brody?'

Her heart started to race with excitement, because he hadn't ordered her out of his condo yet.

'I wouldn't tell him anything. He already loves you and would give anything in the world if I let him spend every spare moment with you. He'd welcome your presence with joy and accept it as a matter of course.'

His head reared back. 'I would never allow a woman to keep me, no matter the circumstances.'

She moistened her lips nervously. 'Since I've already spent the night in your bed, Brody and I might as well move in here with you, then. If you want, you can work out an arrangement to pay my sister and brother-in-law for the use of their condo as an office.'

He stared at her for countless seconds. 'If I took you up on it, you'd run ten thousand miles.'

She got up from the bed and faced him with her final volley. If it didn't work, then she had no idea how to reach him.

'Something tells me you're worried about what all your students and their parents will say when they find out we're living together. Because they *will* find out.'

His hand rubbed his chest absently. 'You think I care about gossip?'

She smoothed a tendril of hair behind her ear. 'I don't know. Something's frightening you off. I guess it's me.' Her shoulders hunched inelegantly. 'Rich was the only man I've ever been with, which probably makes me the most inexperienced woman alive. Apparently *I'm* the one who didn't measure up.' She averted her eyes. 'I feel like a fool.' Even her voice wobbled precariously. 'Please, just forget this conversation ever took place. I'm glad you're better,' she murmured, before dashing out of the room.

She thought she heard him call her name, but she didn't stop running, and flew out the back door to get as far away from him as possible.

Whatever had possessed her to open herself up to Jonah like that? Without meaning to, she'd probably reminded him of his unfaithful wife, the last person in the world Sarah would ever desire to resemble.

Hot tears coursed down her cheeks. Her plan to win Jonah's love had backfired in ways that made her groan in agony. She had to get away for the day and think things out, but she couldn't do that with Brody along.

She called his name as she entered the house, but no one was there. Patsy had left a note on the counter indicating that she'd taken the boys out to breakfast and shopping, that they'd be back around noon.

Since it was only nine-thirty, Sarah had more than two hours to call her own, and could have hugged Patsy for her sensitivity to Sarah's needs. One day soon she'd repay her friend for everything she'd done.

In the meantime, all Sarah wanted to do was get in the car and go. Which was exactly what she did, as soon as she rounded up her purse and keys. She didn't even take time out to wash her face or brush her teeth.

The phone rang several times but she ignored it. If it was an attorney, they'd leave a message. Perhaps it was Patsy, but she doubted it. If by any chance it was Jonah, he was the last person she wanted to talk to right now.

Unfortunately, after a hundred miles of aimless driving, Sarah was still tormented by her encounter with Jonah. She had no conception of how to deal with him from this point on and dreaded seeing him again.

Bracing herself for the inevitable interrogation from Brody, as well as Jeff's parents, she drove by the Masons' condo to pick up her son. After a brief explanation, in which she assured them that Jonah was going to be fine, she thanked them for their help and took Brody home.

He wanted to run over and visit Jonah, but she warned him that Jonah had a bad cold and needed his rest. If left alone, she said, he'd probably be able to teach school on Monday.

To distract her son, she gave him a model airplane and some cement glue which she'd purchased on her drive. The constructions was easy enough that he could follow the directions.

Delighted with his present, Brody spent the better part of the weekend working on it so he could take it to school and show Jonah.

Sarah kept busy cleaning and doing research until she dropped into bed at night. It set a precedent for the rest of the month, three weekends of which she took Jeff with her and Brody to Fort Collins.

There'd been a bombing incident involving a rare books swindle, and a new law firm she hadn't worked for before had got in touch with her. Sarah's job was to show a picture of a man to every rare books dealer in the area to find out if the person in the photo had ever done business there, and, if so, to determine the nature of it.

While she was thus occupied, a licensed babysitter hired by the hotel kept an eye on the boys, who spent most of their time in the indoor pool.

So much work turned out to be a blessing for Sarah, but as the time for Halloween approached she became nervous and jittery at the thought of seeing Jonah again. Though he hadn't come near, she still cringed every time she thought of the things she'd said to him.

As room mothers, she and Lynette would be expected to help with the Halloween parade. And of course there was the class party afterward in Jonah's room. Brody and his friends had decided to go as vampires, which gave Sarah the idea to dress as Vampira.

For some reason, she felt better at the idea of taking on another persona before she faced him. She already had long black hair. All she had to do was powder her skin and wear blood-red lipstick.

Several days before the big event she took Brody to the fabric store, and they bought enough black material for both costumes. She found a couple of patterns which would work and got busy sewing. Soon they both had long black outfits which reached the floor and capes to match, with stand-up collars she had stiffened with wire.

To complete the effect, she bought black hair-spray to apply along their foreheads to form widow's peaks. That, plus fake red fangs and fake black fingernails, completed the picture. When they stood in the front of her mirror on Halloween morning, they actually scared each other.

Sarah was secretly thrilled at the transformation, which she felt gave her an edge with Jonah. For the whole day, she could act the part of Vampira. Hopefully she'd get through it without incident.

Gathering up their contribution to the party of a dozen doughnuts decorated with orange and black frosting, which Brody had picked out, they drove over to school.

Halloween was one of Sarah's favorite holidays. She loved seeing all the children dressed up in everything from bumble bee outfits to dinosaurs. Brody ran off as soon as he saw his fellow cohorts with fake blood dripping from their mouths.

With a chuckle, Sarah walked through the hall to Jonah's classroom, bracing herself for the moment when she saw him. But the only adult who greeted her vision was Lynette, impossible to miss in her Wonder Woman outfit. She showed so much cleavage for Jonah's benefit that Sarah wouldn't have been surprised if the principal had sent her home to change.

So far there was no sign of Jonah. Sarah experienced a mixture of relief and desolation, but she didn't have time to speculate on where he might be because it seemed every child had a problem that needed fixing, especially those with parts to their costumes that kept falling off or needed pinning.

When she heard screams coming from the hall, she dropped what she was doing and ran to the doorway to find out what was going on.

A long way down the corridor she could see a Frankenstein monster coming her way on stilts. The size alone could only belong to one man.

Jonah.

Her heart started to thud heavily in her chest until she thought she'd be sick.

While the younger children shrieked in fear, the older ones cheered and shouted in fascinated delight and followed his progress. He'd stuffed a hideous dark gray outfit so that it made him look exactly like the monster in the old Bela Lugosi film.

Every teacher in the building had congregated in the hall to watch the frightening apparition. Someone had a camera and a flash went off.

She could tell the second Jonah saw her. He made a snarling, half-crazed sound and started in her direction. The menacing way he approached her so swiftly on those stilts terrified her. She shrank back into the room, terrified in more ways than one, and found refuge with half a dozen children.

Thankfully, he had to get down from his stilts to enter the class. Even so he looked huge, and made such a horrifying sight it caused everyone to give him wide berth, even Lynette.

Sarah immediately busied herself fixing a braid which had come undone on a Raggedy Ann character. When she'd finished her task, she looked up and realized Jonah was lumbering up to her, exactly like the monster. She could see his piercing gaze riveted fully on her through the eye-slits. She tried to swallow, but couldn't.

'We make quite a pair,' he murmured in that deep, rich voice which no longer sounded congested. 'If you don't come around by midnight to take a bite out of me, I intend to break down your back door and carry you off, so be warned.'

Lynette and some of the children couldn't have helped but hear him, which made Sarah wonder if he was simply playing out a part for everyone's entertainment. But the predatory gleam in his eye sent chills racing across her skin, forcing her to revise that opinion.

After a whole month of not seeing or hearing from him, she couldn't understand his about-face and decided she was reading far too much into it.

'Do you think that would be wise?' she answered him in her best Bela Lugosi imitation. 'Once bitten, you have to become my slave and do my bidding.' She bared her fake red fangs to him and hissed.

'You know what they say about nothing risked.'

On that cryptic note he headed for his desk while Sarah stood there trembling. Was he saying what she thought he was saying?

From that moment on, Sarah was a mass of nerves, incapable of concentrating on anything. Her heart kept acting up until she thought she must be quite ill.

Out of the corner of her eye she regarded Jonah, who finally pulled off his rubber face-mask so the students would relax and start laughing and talking to him. The transformation from Frankenstein to Apollo was nothing short of miraculous.

Brody stuck to him like glue. When it came time for the parade, he and his friends edged out Lynette to walk directly behind Jonah's stilts. Slowly the children began shuffling through the halls in all their finery toward the auditorium.

The rest of the day passed by in a blur of activity. Though she never again spoke to Jonah, who was monopolized by Lynette during the class party, his comments haunted her and the hours passed by far too slowly.

At six that evening, Brody and his friends were ready to go trick-or-treating. They'd already been over to Jonah's and he'd given them chocolate peanut butter cups, Brody's favorite candy.

After some discussion it was decided that Patsy would take the boys for the first hour, when they would canvass one half of the complex and end up at Kevin's. From there, his mom would take them for another hour to finish up the rest of the condos and arrive at Sarah's; she had agreed to take the boys to Birchwood South for as long as they could hold out.

Once they'd gone, Sarah set one of the speakers to the stereo on the window ledge and opened the window. Then she put in a tape of spooky music with eerie sound-effects and turned it up as loud as she could stand.

After she had lighted the carved pumpkin on the front porch, the one Brody had made in class under Jonah's supervision, she filled a plastic witch's pot with bite-size candy bars and set it by the front door.

She'd barely had time to repair her Vampira make-up when the buzzer sounded. One after another, big and little nocturnal creatures appeared on her doorstep.

Since this was her first Halloween in Denver, she had no idea how many children to expect and was glad she'd bought extra bags of candy to feed the mob.

At eight o'clock she heard the back buzzer. Figuring it was Brody, she walked through the kitchen to the door and called out to him. But all she heard was a growl, and her legs almost buckled.

'Jonah?' she cried out in alarm. 'I-Is that you?' There was another ferocious snarl followed by a hair-raising scratch on the screen. Maybe it wasn't Jonah. 'I won't open up unless you identify yourself.'

When there was no answer she purposely left the kitchen and headed for the living-room. She'd barely reached it when she saw the head of the Frankenstein monster outside the screened-in-open window. She couldn't help letting out a blood-curdling scream, even though she knew Jonah's handsome face was underneath that hideous mask.

'I've come for my bite. Let me in, Sarah, or your neighbors will be calling 911.'

Half-faint with excitement, she opened the door with shaky fingers and received her second shock of the evening when he lunged for her.

'Wh-What are you doing?' she asked, totally out of breath because he'd planted himself on the top step of the porch, forcing her to sit on his lap.

'While we wait for Brody, I'll keep you warm,' he vowed in husky tones, and nuzzled the rubber of his mask against the side of her neck while he wrapped her in his huge arms.

No sooner had he created this spectacle, which made every child in the street come over and talk to them, than Brody and his friends arrived. In his exuberance at seeing Jonah holding Sarah, he threw himself into her arms, almost causing the three of them to overbalance.

To her surprise, Jonah gave in to the boys' pleadings to join them trick-or-treating over at the other complex, but only on the condition that Sarah went with them.

After a month of not being with him, she could hardly believe this was happening, and fell in with his wishes immediately.

While Jonah put out the candle in the pumpkin, she grabbed her purse and locked up the house. They left in his car for another half-hour of fun. When it was all over, Jonah delivered the boys to their various houses, then turned to Sarah, his mask still on.

'How would you and Brody like to come to my house? We'll watch videos and call out for pizza?'

'Can we, Mom?' Brody asked, his heart in his eyes.

'I was going to suggest it myself.'

'Hooray!'

'But I think we'd better go back to our condo first and wash off our make-up.'

'Yeah. It's itchy.'

Jonah chuckled. 'I'll go with you, to make sure you're both safe.'

There was almost a possessive ring to his words, filling Sarah's heart to overflowing.

Something told her that this night was going to change her life and Brody's.

CHAPTER TEN

HALFWAY through Disney's *Watcher in the Woods*, Brody conked out. After eating several pieces of pizza, he'd found his way to Jonah's lap, while Sarah had made herself comfortable on one of the upholstered couches.

With that grace and economy of movement peculiar to Jonah, he got up and placed Brody on the other couch, covering him with a blanket he'd brought in from the bedroom.

The moment had come which Sarah had been impatiently waiting for. Her heart was pounding far too fast and her cheeks felt hot. She couldn't blame her skin's reaction to the make-up for their fiery glow.

As the silence grew and stretched between them, she started to get nervous. The funning of Halloween was definitely over.

It was a remote, taciturn Jonah who turned in her direction, his features sharply etched in the shadowy light, as if he'd finished wrestling with a problem that had taken its toll.

'I'm glad he's asleep, because there's something I have to tell you.'

Alert to the nuance of impending disaster in his voice, her body tautened. 'It sounds serious.'

'I'm afraid so.'

Unable to sit still, Sarah got to her feet, rubbing her arms nervously. 'Are you ill again?' She asked the first question that entered her mind.

'No. I've told you. My recurring bouts of fever are not life-threatening.'

'It didn't look that way to me,' she came back, a trifle too angrily.

He appeared to digest her outburst, but let it pass. 'I've accomplished what I set out to do with my experiment, and have decided to cut my teaching career short. A fully qualified second grade teacher has been found to take over until Mrs Ruff comes back.'

If Sarah had been stabbed repeatedly with a knife, the pain and shock of it couldn't have been any greater.

When Jonah had invited them over she hadn't known what to expect, but she'd never dreamed the evening would end up anything like this.

Through wooden lips she said, 'When are you leaving?'

'I'm driving to San Diego in the morning.'

Dear God.

'I've alerted the landlord that the movers will be coming to pack up my things. I wanted you to know ahead of time so you could explain to Brody.'

'Explain *what*——?' she raged in a barely controlled voice. 'That his idol had to leave town unexpectedly and won't be back?'

His features hardened. 'This day had to come, even I can see that, so I'm leaving now, before he gets too——' He paused before adding, 'Attached.'

'*Attached——*' she almost shouted. 'He loves you!' Her voice throbbed.

'In time he'll learn to love someone else. A clean break is always best.'

His insensitive comment, after everything they'd been through and experienced together, put the last nail in the coffin.

She stood there in a trance-like state.

Four weeks ago she'd tossed all pride to the wind and had offered herself to Jonah. She'd literally thrown herself at him, gone down on her knees to him, because she'd been so in love with him.

Her feelings hadn't changed. If anything, they'd grown stronger. In fact, she had the horrifying conviction that no other man would ever touch her heart again and she'd go through the rest of her life alone, with Brody her only joy.

But Jonah's cold detachment filled her veins with ice. She stared straight at him, despising the woman who'd turned him into an emotional cripple.

No one will ever love you the way I do, Jonah Sinclair. We could have had it all.

While the death-knell sounded in her heart, she said in a bright, brittle tone, 'You're right. This *is* the best way to handle it. Let's get him home to bed. If you'll carry him, I'll run on ahead and open the door.'

Not waiting to hear whether he liked the idea or not, she fled his condo and raced along the access drive as if demons were at her heels.

By the time Jonah came through the back entrance of her condo, with Brody in his arms, Sarah was on the phone listening to any business messages that might have come while she'd been out. 'Just lie him on top of the mattress and put a quilt over him,' she instructed in a well-modulated tone while she recorded a couple of phone numbers.

Obviously Brody was out for the count, because Jonah came back to the kitchen almost immediately.

When he seemed to hesitate she said, 'Thanks,' and continued to write down some information one of the attorneys had left with her. When Jonah still didn't leave, she called over her shoulder, 'Have a good trip home.'

'*Sarah*——' He jerked the receiver out of her hand and slammed it down in the cradle. 'Stop being so damn cheerful and look at me!'

If he didn't get out of there, she was going to lose it. Fighting for her life, she turned an expressionless façade to him. 'You always do the right thing, so why all this passion?'

His hands tightened into fists at his sides, letting her know he wasn't as in control as she'd thought. It was something to treasure in the empty years ahead.

He searched her face relentlessly. 'Are you going to be all right?'

His question threw her, because it was underscored by some unnamed emotion he hadn't been able to hide. Something else to cherish.

'I won't pretend that dealing with Brody's disappointment won't be a major hurdle, but, as you once said, people he loves will always be coming and going in his life. One of these days he'll get over it and form an attachment to someone else. Who knows, maybe your replacement will be his next fixation?'

His chest heaved. 'I wasn't talking about Brody.'

She flashed him a guileless smile. 'If you think I'm going to fall apart because you're leaving, then think again. Rich's death cured me of believing anything lasts forever.'

She couldn't be positive, but she thought his face had lost a little of its color.

'You're an extraordinary human being, Jonah. Brody and I have been lucky to get to know you as well as we have. Every time we look up at the stars, we'll remember that there was once a man who taught us about heaven.'

Propelling herself to the door, she opened it and clung to the knob.

'Lynette tells me she's planning to spend Thanksgiving in San Diego with you. Do Brody a big favor and ask Lynette not to broadcast it to the world after she returns to Denver. Like her mother, Talia enjoys the sensational, and she could do real damage by rubbing it in.' Her voice shook with emotion she could no longer hide.

'Goodbye, Jonah. Good luck.'

'Has the mailman come?' Brody asked the second he walked in the kitchen from school, his parka dusted with snow.

'He has. There are a couple of fun new Christmas cards in the basket.' Sarah looked up from the gingerbread men she was cutting out to eye her son. Like *déjà vu*, Brody had resorted to watching for a letter from Jonah, just the way he had used to wait for some word from his grandparents, which had never come and never would.

So far she'd barely kept the lid on Brody's depressed mental state, and dreaded the next two weeks because school was finally out for the holidays. Now he'd go to his room and brood for eighteen hours a day. She couldn't bear the thought.

The Monday after Halloween, when he'd learned that Jonah wasn't at school because he'd had to go back to California for business reasons, he had taken the news more calmly than Sarah would have expected. But that was because he had thought Jonah's absence was temporary.

It wasn't until the following week, when the new teacher announced that Jonah wouldn't be able to come back at all due to the demands of his work, that Brody fell apart.

He left class without permission and ran all the way home, throwing himself into Sarah's arms so heartbroken she had to fight not to break down and sob with him. In the state he was in, there was no question of his going back to school.

On the advice of her pediatrician, she took Brody to a child psychiatrist, who, when she heard his whole history, which included the death of his father, helped him get through the next month and calmed him down enough to cope with school.

So far Sarah hadn't felt he'd regressed to the point that she needed to take him back, but that was because school had kept his mind occupied. Now that it was out, she wasn't so sure.

Thank heavens Sylvia and her daughters were coming. Sarah was expecting them the next afternoon. She'd saved all the decorating until Brody could help her, so that they'd have so much to do neither of them would be able to indulge in fantasies too painful even to entertain.

One bright spot had been a phone call from Mrs Ruff, who'd had her baby and was planning on being back at school after New Year's Day.

She had advised all the parents that on Christmas Eve her husband would be coming around to each condo, playing Santa Claus to all the children in her class. It was a tradition they'd started several years back. She wanted to give each of them a little treat she'd made and more or less prepare them for her re-entry into their lives.

Sarah decided that a live visit from Santa Claus was exactly what her house needed to prevent Christmas from being a sad occasion. Sylvia's girls would be delighted and maybe, by some miracle, it would bring a smile to Brody's face.

Though Sylvia had begged Sarah not to bother coming to the airport, Sarah had insisted. It would get Brody out of the house and possibly help him catch some of the Christmas spirit as they passed all the houses and shops decorated for the holidays.

A recent snowstorm had arrived in time to make everything look fresh and beautiful. Sarah was determined to make this a festive occasion. And there was another reason to be happy, because Sarah's sister and brother-in-law might be coming home sooner than they'd originally planned, which meant that Brody could help her find a new place to live which wouldn't have all the old, attendant memories. It would be their own home, one that would still be close by, so that Brody could visit his friends.

Fortunately for Sarah, word was getting around that she was a good researcher. More and more business was being thrown her way, and several attorneys had given her bonuses for Christmas—enough to help her buy Brody a pair of ice-skates and a sled.

She still didn't have enough money to purchase the kind of telescope he kept praying for when he talked to God about Jonah. It was just as well, since they didn't need that particular reminder at this precarious stage in their lives.

After Sylvia's family had been at her house for a couple of days, Sarah could see a change in all of them. They seemed to be happier, more well-adjusted. Brody, on the other hand, wasn't doing nearly as well. Even Sylvia commented on it, and finally Sarah broke down to explain about Jonah.

Sylvia commiserated with Sarah's problem and promised to do everything she could to help. They filled their days with shopping at the malls, ice-skating, movies. Though Brody showed little enthusiasm, he went along with everything. By the time Christmas Eve arrived, Sarah was beginning to think maybe they'd get through this holiday without too much trauma.

Throughout the evening, they ate turkey and opened a couple of pre-Christmas presents which involved paints and coloring books, something to keep them busy.

Sarah had told Sylvia about Mrs Ruff's phone call so she'd know what to expect. When the front buzzer finally sounded, their eyes met in a secret message of understanding.

Unable to concentrate totally on anything these days, Brody was the first one to his feet. He ran to the door to answer it. His actions tugged at Sarah's heart because she knew that deep down inside of him he prayed it would be Jonah. How many years would this go on? she agonized.

First she heard sleigh bells, then, 'Ho! Ho! Ho! Merry Christmas!' A deep, jovial voice resounded in the living-room ahead of the most perfect-looking Santa Claus Sarah had ever seen in her life.

He came bounding inside with a huge pack on his back.

Even Brody couldn't remain immune to such a wondrous sight. Mrs Ruff's husband was obviously tall and strong. Sarah had no idea how much of that large belly belonged to him, but, as far as she was concerned, he had made Christmas for them.

Sarah found herself studying him as he found himself a comfortable chair by the fireplace, where a couple of Presto logs were burning. With great ceremony he sat down, his legs apart, and called the girls over one at a time to sit on his lap so he could ask them the usual questions.

He had a certain way about him that inspired confidence in the children, much like another man she had once known. But she couldn't afford to think about him anymore.

After Santa had made them giggle, he reached in his pack and gave each of them a candy cane and a white envelope. Inside each was a felt ornament representing one of the twelve days of Christmas. Sarah marveled at Mrs Ruff's generosity and creative talent.

Then came Brody's turn. With an encouraging smile on her face for her son, Sarah urged him to take his place on Santa's lap. Though he wasn't jumping up and down as he had used to do—before the two men he loved most in the world had gone out of his life forever—he did show some signs of wanting to take a turn.

She noticed that Mrs Ruff's husband was sensitive to Brody's timidity, and simply gestured with a finger for him to climb up on his lap.

Finally Brody gave in and walked over to him, sitting stiffly on his leg without looking at the face hidden behind the fluffy white beard and mustache.

When he asked him what he wanted for Christmas, Brody answered, 'A telescope, 'cause my mom can't afford one.'

Sarah sent Sylvia a worried glance.

'A telescope, hmm?' He handed Brody an envelope and a candy cane. 'What do you want one of those for?'

'To look at heaven.'

'Hmm,' Santa pondered out loud. 'Well, now. I'll have to think about that one. In the meantime, let's get your moms over here.'

The children clapped in delight as Sylvia took her turn and received the same gifts as the children. Then it came time for Sarah, who took her place where the others had sat.

'What's your name?' Santa asked her. When she told him, he said, 'Well, Sarah, your son says you don't have enough money to get him a telescope. I think maybe I can do something about that.'

He reached in his pack and pulled out an identical envelope and candy cane for her. Sarah thanked him for the gifts.

No sooner had she moved off him than their visitor stood up, bellowed out, 'Merry Christmas!' and departed. The sleigh bells around his middle jangled as he moved. She could still hear them after Brody closed the door.

All of sudden he ran over to her. 'Did Santa give you some money to buy me a telescope?'

'I don't think so, honey.'

'Can I open it? Please?'

She didn't have the heart to refuse him. 'Go ahead.'

With an eagerness she hadn't seen since he'd climbed on Jonah's lap to watch the Halloween movie, he ripped open the envelope and pulled out an ornament. There was an accompanying note, but no money. Sarah could have told him there wouldn't be any.

'Oh, heck.' He dropped everything in her lap and went back to his coloring book on the floor.

Taking a fortifying breath, Sarah picked up the card Mrs Ruff had included, and read it.

Dear Mrs Brown,

Arrived in Denver December twenty-fourth, at one pm. There was no need to pick me up at the airport because I drove my car instead. It's parked in its usual spot. Feel free to drop by my condo at any time for your gifts.

Jonah.

P.S. I love you. I want to spend the rest of my life with you. I want to change your name from Brown to Sinclair as soon as possible, preferably before we see the New Year in together. All three of us.

Sarah stood up too fast and the blood left her head. She clung to the back of the sofa until the world stopped swimming and her heart slowed down enough for her to talk.

'Sylvia?'

At the sound of her name, which came out more like a squeak, Sarah's friend, who'd been putting the ornaments on the tree, turned around with a puzzled expression in her eyes.

'What's wrong? You look like you've seen a ghost.'

'I—I've just heard from one,' she whispered emotionally. 'Will you please keep an eye on the children for a minute? I have to run to the condo a couple of doors down for a little while. Don't say anything to Brody.'

Sylvia shook her head. 'No. I won't. Sarah, are you all right?'

'I think I will be in a few minutes.'

Sarah didn't stop to put on her boots or coat. She never remembered anything about her flight out the back door and through the snow.

'Jonah?' she shouted at the top of her lungs when she came in sight of his condo and saw the Jaguar in its stall. '*Jonah*?' she cried again, louder than before, afraid maybe she was dreaming this.

'I'm right here, darling. I've been waiting for you,' he murmured, in that deep, vibrant voice that sent shivers of ecstasy through her body.

He stepped unexpectedly from the car, wearing dark trousers and a turtleneck sweater. In a lightning move he caught her in his arms, lifting her high in the air before he crushed her against his heart and lowered his mouth to hers.

Sarah couldn't believe this was happening, that this was Jonah kissing her, devouring her until she felt that they had become one living, breathing entity, aching for the fulfillment of a need only they could assuage.

'If you only knew——' She tried getting the words out.

'Tell me about it.' He captured her mouth over and over again, not giving her a chance to breathe let alone tell him everything that was in her heart. Unaware of time and place, Sarah gave herself up to the divine glory of loving and being loved by him.

He carried her inside the condo, but they only made it as far as the kitchen, because no kiss was long enough or deep enough. They needed each other's closeness so desperately they couldn't bear to move another inch.

'When did you realize that I loved you?' she managed to ask him when he finally allowed her to talk.

His hands gripped her shoulders almost painfully. 'I think I always knew it, somewhere deep in my gut, but I was afraid to trust my feelings. You were just getting over your husband's death, and I was still trying to reconcile my wife's betrayal. When you suggested that we live together, I got my first inkling that you were dead serious. It terrified me because I wanted it so badly, but I had made a promise to myself that I wouldn't get anymore involved with you.'

'Why?' she cried, still remembering the pain as if it were yesterday.

'You're so young, so beautiful, Sarah. Any man would desire you. Any man could give you more children. I felt it would be selfish to take what you were offering, because I couldn't give you anything in return.'

Her hands cupped his face. 'Not give me anything Jonah—— You don't know what you're saying. You're my whole life, my reason for being——' Tears ran unashamedly down her cheeks. 'I already have a son who worships the ground you walk on. We'll adopt more. There are children in the world who are in desperate need of a father like you. There's a woman——' her voice trembled '—who's in desperate need of a husband like you.'

Her brilliant blue eyes gazed at him in adoration.

'She's right here, darling, ready to be all things to you. Don't you know I've wanted to be Mrs Sinclair since the day you came in from the rain, transforming my life?'

'*Sarah*—— Dear God, how I love you. Hold me, darling. Love me. Love me,' he begged, crushing her mouth once more until she was clinging to him, leaving him in no doubt that this was the place she was meant to be.

'Mom?'

At the sound of Brody's anxious voice outside the door Jonah reluctantly tore his lips from hers, leaving them both reeling from the power of their overflowing emotions.

'Answer the door,' she whispered, giving him another sensuous kiss before letting him go.

He grabbed her around the waist and they moved to the entry together, and he opened it.

After a stunned silence his little voice rang with joy, his face a shining light. '*Jonah*! *You're back*!'

Sarah put a hand over her heart, to ease the pain of too much happiness. Miracles *did* come true on Christmas Day.

'That's right.' She heard a catch in Jonah's husky voice. 'I'm home to stay.' He held out his arms. 'Come here, son.'

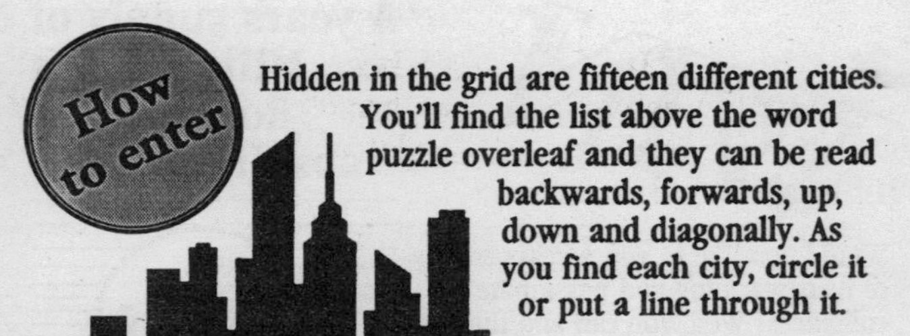

Hidden in the grid are fifteen different cities. You'll find the list above the word puzzle overleaf and they can be read backwards, forwards, up, down and diagonally. As you find each city, circle it or put a line through it.

When you have found all fifteen, don't forget to fill in your name and address in the space provided below and pop this page in an envelope (you don't need a stamp) and post it today. Hurry – competition ends 30th April 1996.

Mills & Boon Capital Wordsearch
FREEPOST
Croydon
Surrey
CR9 3WZ

Are you a Reader Service Subscriber? Yes ❑ No ❑

Ms/Mrs/Miss/Mr ______________________________

Address ______________________________

____

______________ Postcode ______________

One application per household.

You may be mailed with other offers from other reputable companies as a result of this application. If you would prefer not to receive such offers, please tick box. ❑

COMP495
D